D0975408

A Cup of
CHRISTMAS
CHEER

VOLUME FOUR

A Cup of
CHRISTMAS
CHEER

HEARTWARMING TALES *of*
CHRISTMAS PRESENT

Guideposts
New York

A Cup of Christmas Cheer is a trademark of Guideposts.

Published by Guideposts Books & Inspirational Media
110 William Street
New York, NY 10038
Guideposts.org

Acknowledgments

Every attempt has been made to credit the sources of copyrighted material used
in this book. If any such acknowledgment has been inadvertently omitted or
miscredited, receipt of such information would be appreciated.

Cover and interior design by Müllerhaus
Illustrated by Greg Copeland, represented by Deborah Wolfe, LTD
Typeset by Aptara

Printed and bound in the United States of America
10 9 8 7 6 5 4 3 2 1

CONTENTS

THE TWELVE DAYS OF KINDNESS

Jenness Walker

*I*t's all Brian's fault.

Tonya Rutherford rehearsed the words in her head in case they got caught. Her brother had been the one to find the Christmas gifts hidden in the hall closet, after all. Maybe *she* had happened to mention that Mom wouldn't be home for another hour and Dad was busy shoveling the driveway, but at twelve, Brian was the oldest by two years and oh, how he loved to rub that in.

Well, with age came responsibility. And blame. So the fact that they were currently digging through the presents—checking tags before ripping free the wrapping—was totally Brian's fault.

When Mom came home early and found them, that was exactly what Tonya told her. Before she could explain, however, she and a glowering Brian were shuttled off to their rooms to "think about what you've done."

Opening presents early did ruin the Christmas morning surprise, but it also gave Tonya time to decide where her new toys should go and to brainstorm ways to talk Dad into buying a RipStik skateboard for her too. Brian shouldn't have all the fun.

"Tonya!" Brian whispered from across the hall.

"What?" she hissed back.

"It was half your fault and you know it. When Mom comes, you better tell her."

That wasn't going to happen. Tonya ignored the rest of his rumblings and pulled out her journal.

> *Dear Journal,*
>   *This year I'm getting my own box of chocolate-covered cherries. Dad usually shares, but I guess I'm all grown up now! Let's see, what else? A new game for the Wii. Some clothes. A Barbie. Those new books I've been wanting with the horses. A horse calendar. Hmm...maybe a few other things. And best of all, that red coat I wanted with the big, shiny buttons.*

TONYA WAS STUCK IN HER ROOM FOREVER. AT LEAST long enough to lay out an outfit for her new Barbie, reread the beginning of *Black Beauty*, and watch Mrs. Foley across the street try to untangle the leash of her puffball pet from her walker.

Finally Mom knocked on the open door, looking somber. "Come to the living room. We're ready to discuss what you've done."

Tonya trudged behind her, bracing for the coming judgment. Brian followed Dad into the room a moment later. Being grounded wouldn't be too bad with school ending soon and everyone going away. If she was assigned extra chores, she could just picture what she was working toward, like the pretty red coat, and if she did a better job than Brian, maybe they'd swap out her Wii game for the RipStik with her brother's name on it.

The gifts were spread on the floor. Tonya sat on the couch and studied them all again.

"These were to be your Christmas gifts," Mom said with a slight tremble in her voice. "We love to see you happy, which is one reason we love to give you gifts."

Dad set an empty box on the coffee table. "Another reason is because they represent what God did for us on the first Christmas. He loved us, so He sent a special gift—the most *priceless* gift."

Tonya knew this, of course. "He sent Jesus."

"That's right, Tonya."

Mom set down a second box.

"Not good." Brian muttered, sending another glare Tonya's way.

"But," Mom said, "we're afraid you two have forgotten something Jesus said when He grew up."

"Really not good," Brian repeated.

What was he talking about?

"Jesus said it's more blessed to give than to receive." Dad picked up the RipStik. Maybe Tonya was getting it after all? "To make sure you two understand that important lesson, this year will be all about giving. There will be no receiving."

The RipStik went into one box. The Wii game followed close behind.

"You're returning our presents?" Brian asked.

In answer, Dad wrote on the cardboard in big black letters: *Return*.

Tonya bit her lip. No red coat, no chocolates, no nothing? But wait. She'd opened the Barbie. They couldn't return that.

As she watched, the doll went into the other box. Mom took the marker from Dad to write *Donate*.

This couldn't be happening.

Dad placed another toy in the Return box, then picked up the red coat. "You forfeited Christmas gifts this year. Instead, you will be giving to others."

Mom leveled her eyes on Brian, then turned to Tonya. "Each day—*including* today—through Christmas Eve, you are to do something kind for another person. A *different* person each time."

"Twelve Days of Kindness." Dad smiled. "A new kind of Christmas countdown."

Tonya put her head in her hands. So. Not. Fair.

"How do we know what to do?" Brian asked. "Especially after everyone leaves on vacation."

Mom and Dad exchanged looks. "You'll figure something out," Dad said. "Just try to think about others instead of yourselves." He ruffled Brian's hair, then rested his hand on Tonya's head. "This isn't easy for us either. We carefully chose those gifts, and we don't want to seem cruel, but this is an important lesson you need to learn to help you become the amazing people we know you can be."

Tonya groaned inwardly at this version of the "it hurts me worse than it hurts you" speech.

Brian turned to her and mouthed, "You're dead."

BACK IN HER ROOM, TONYA OPENED HER JOURNAL AND pulled out her purple pen. But her page remained as blank as her mind. There was no one Tonya wanted to be nice to at the moment. Who would, when they knew there wouldn't be any Christmas presents?

Then she remembered hearing about all the orphans who probably *never* got Christmas presents. But they weren't here, where all her friends would come back to school showing off their new stuff.

Tonya crept across the hall to Brian's room.

He scowled. "What do you want?"

"What are you going to do today?"

"None of your business."

"But I need help."

"You threw me under the bus."

"Did not."

"Did too."

Tonya sighed. "Maybe a little."

"The fact that I'm talking to you should count as my good deed—maybe for the whole week."

Brian would be no help. Shoulders slumped, Tonya left his room and spent the rest of the day trying to come up with something to do. But all she could think about were the presents that *wouldn't* be under the tree this year.

Before bed, Tonya carried her useless journal to the kitchen and made hot cocoa, hoping the chocolate would give a spark of inspiration.

Brian wandered in as the microwave dinged. "Is there any left?"

"Are you blind?" Tonya motioned to the packets, pulled out her mug, and mixed in the cocoa. Then she found the bag of marshmallows. It was mostly empty. Popping one in her mouth, she waited for her cup to cool.

She should take what was left of the marshmallows— after all, hot cocoa had been her idea, and Brian deserved to miss out after today's fiasco. But it was almost bedtime and her journal page was blank. Plus, who wanted marshmallows? They were sticky. Gooey. Messy.

But they tasted so good.

With a long-suffering sigh, Tonya placed the bag beside the microwave, picked up her mug, and padded to her room.

> *Dear Journal,*
>
> *Countdown to Christmas, Day 12:*
>
> *I let Brian have all the marshmallows. Hopefully he'll appreciate the sacrifice...but he probably won't even notice.*

"DID YOU KIDDOS DO SOMETHING KIND YESTERDAY?" Mom placed a basket of fresh-baked goodies on the table.

Brian gave a slow nod as he took two muffins. If he meant speaking to Tonya, that *so* did not count.

"Tonya?"

She didn't want to talk to Mom. Partly because she was angry, partly because she didn't like having Mom look at her the way she did yesterday. Like she was disappointed.

"Did you do it, Tonya?"

"Yes." She threw a look at Brian. "I gave—"

"No, don't tell me." Mom held up a hand, then lowered it, looking thoughtful. "As much as I want to leave you both to follow through with your assignment, yesterday proved you're not completely trustworthy. However, acts of kindness shouldn't be done for pats on the back, so I don't want you to tell everyone about your good deeds." She drummed her fingers against the table. "How about this: see the calendar on the refrigerator? After you do your good deed, write your initial in the day's square. Your father and I will check it to make sure you're on track. Simple enough?"

They nodded dutifully.

"Good. Now, pray and eat your breakfast. Tonya, after you're done, I'll fix your hair."

WHILE MOM FINESSED TONYA'S BLONDE FRIZZ INTO curls, Tonya doodled in her journal. Maybe she was self-centered after all, because she couldn't think of a single nice thing to do besides dishes, and it was Sunday—Dad's day for kitchen cleanup. So even if she *wanted* to do the dishes, she couldn't take away the nice thing *he* planned to do.

At church, Mrs. Watkins called "Merry Christmas" as she juggled boxes of candy canes while wrestling with the double doors. Before Tonya's brain kicked into gear, Brian jumped up the steps and swung one of the doors open. He stayed there—the unofficial door holder—until just before service started, then slid onto the seat next to Tonya with a smug smile.

"Save it, moron," Tonya said before he could rub it in that he was already done for the day.

The pastor talked about the gifts the wise men brought baby Jesus. Presents, presents everywhere, except under the tree at the Rutherford house. Tonya crossed her arms. It would be easier to give to other people if she knew she was getting something in return.

She brought that up on the way home.

Dad turned in his seat. He didn't need to watch the road—Mom always did that for him. "You can't earn a gift, because then it would be something else: payment. A gift is freely given, just because the giver wants to."

"Get it through your thick skull," Brian muttered. "No presents this year, twerp."

"It's your fault," Tonya whispered.

"Seriously? You're sticking to that?"

"*Mostly* your fault."

"Kids!" Mom said. Then, "Honey, stay in your lane."

Tonya watched cars whiz by. Getting in a wreck before Christmas would stink, but it wasn't like she'd be missing much of a celebration this year.

"I think we all need to spend time focusing on the reason for Christmas," Mom said. "Jesus came to help others. Why don't we try to do the same?"

Easy enough for them to say. They weren't the ones going without presents.

Brian grumbled that Jesus didn't have a sister like Tonya. She stuck out her tongue, then smiled innocently when Dad checked the rearview mirror.

GUILT HIT LATER, AS DAD PLUNGED HIS HANDS INTO soapy dishwater. He was so kind, always doing things for others without complaining and without being asked. When she grew up, she wanted to be like him.

Just not today, and definitely not while he was doing dishes. But maybe she should look for something nice to do, like she was supposed to.

Dear Journal,

   Day 11:

   Mrs. Foley tried walking her dog again, but the dog wanted to go in circles, and that doesn't work when you have to use a walker. So I took Fluffy around the block for her. (Yes, Fluffy. Ugh.)

   While Fluffy was sniffing around, I saw the real estate agent take down the Sold sign in front of the house next door to Mrs. Foley's and drive off with it. Does that mean the new neighbors are finally moving in?

Tonya wrote a *T* on the calendar. It might have been underneath Brian's *B*, but that night she rested her head on the pillow with the satisfaction of knowing that at least it was bigger.

Dear Journal,

Day 10:

At school, everyone talked about what they wanted for Christmas. (Everything.) What they knew they were getting for Christmas. (Almost everything.) And where they were going. (As in Disney World.) Not. Cool.

I taped money to the vending machine and called it a day.

"WHAT'D YOU DO TODAY?" BRIAN MUMBLED AROUND a mouthful of chocolate-covered pretzels.

"None of your business. You'd better leave some for me."

"You haven't done it yet, have you?"

"Yes, I have." Tonya ran to her room and returned with a sparkly sticker, which she stuck on the calendar. Now he couldn't miss it. "See?"

"You didn't leave room for me."

"That's because *you* didn't do anything."

"Did too. I gave Isabel my apple."

"Doesn't count."

"Why not?"

"Because you like Isabel, and you don't like apples."

"Do not!"

"See?"

He blushed.

"So it doesn't count."

"Well, yours doesn't either."

"Why not?"

"Because you walked Mrs. Foley's dog yesterday. Can't do the same thing twice. That's the rule."

"I did something else."

"Sure."

"I did!" Tonya put her hands on her hips. "I left my snack money at the vending machine!"

A strange smile spread across his face. "That was you?"

"Yeah. Told you."

He laughed, then dropped onto the floor and laughed harder.

"What's so funny?"

"*I* found the money. I used it to replace my apple."

Dear Journal,
　　This project stinks.

TUESDAY WAS A PERFECT DAY FOR READING BY THE Christmas tree, *not* sitting in art class, making a sad-looking Christmas card and watching the seconds tick toward library hour.

Tonya glued on the last glittered ornament and stared at her handiwork. Not awful, but not great. Shoving the card to the corner of the desk, Tonya made room for her stack of books to return to the library. Next came the journal, with a blank page for the day. So far, no opportunities to be nice had presented themselves. But soon she could forget about it for a while as she went to her favorite class. Last week hadn't been as fun, since there'd been a substitute librarian. Miss Patrick's dad had died, but surely she'd be back by now.

Tonya sighed. What a horrible time for someone to die. Even if Miss Patrick's dad hadn't taken away *her* gifts, the librarian must be so sad. Tonya ruffled the pages of her journal, wishing she could help.

The ugly card caught her eye, and she bit her lip. It was the thought that counted, right? She opened it and wrote a note in her neatest handwriting. When finished, she tucked her favorite bookmark inside and sealed the envelope.

Dear Journal,
> *Day 9:*
> *While I have many talents, arts and crafts is not one of them. If the note doesn't cheer Miss Patrick up, maybe my lack of artistic abilities will make her laugh. (If that last glob of glitter and glue doesn't stick the whole thing together.)*

Tonya wrinkled her nose. Maybe she should have let it dry a little longer.

Class dismissed. She gathered her things, headed to library, and greeted Miss Patrick. There. Another day with another initial on the calendar, and this time she'd make sure she didn't leave room for Brian's *B*. Just because.

Even better than annoying Brian was the smile on Miss Patrick's face as she took the card. Her hug warmed Tonya all the way to her pinky toes.

Dear Journal,
> *Maybe the project isn't so horrible after all.*
> *(But I still want my presents.)*

As soon as school dismissed Wednesday, Tonya ran to Mrs. Foley's house to walk Fluffy. Freezing rain was in the forecast, and the dainty little cat-dog didn't like to get wet. Mrs. Foley thanked Tonya and sent her off with a candy cane. Tonya sucked on it while she walked, lost in thought. Today had been a whirlwind of program practices and celebrations, without much of a chance for her to consider options for today's good deed.

Fluffy didn't count, of course. She'd already done something for Brian—twice, by accident. Hopefully that vending machine fiasco wouldn't cause a problem. Unless she found someone to help soon, she'd be stuck doing something for Mom. Or Dad. And though she wasn't still angry—not really—it was hard to want to do something special for them when there were two overflowing, Sharpie-marked boxes in the back of Mom's van.

Maybe she should tell Dad.

Tonya remembered the calendar. *Or maybe I could just do it myself.*

Dear Journal,

Day 8

I made coffee today. Put it in a Thermos, dug out foam cups, and hoped for the best. I'm not sure that was a good deed, considering it was my first coffee-making attempt and it was unsupervised. But I added a plate of Mom's chocolate-dipped chocolate chip cookies, so that should make up for any damages.

Tonya snitched another cookie off the kitchen table and chewed as she replayed the afternoon. The new family who had moved in next to Mrs. Foley had been surprised to see her, grateful for the goodies, and—best news ever—they had a daughter. The girl had stayed inside the house, wrapped in blankets, huddled on the couch. She was pretty, with a big smile and brown eyes.

"Hi. I'm Joelle, and I'm eleven," she had said.

"I'm Tonya, and I'm ten and a half. I live down the street. Did anyone ever tell you your eyes look like Bambi's?"

Joelle laughed and blushed. "It's my hair—it sets them off."

"You might be right." Joelle didn't have any hair. None at all.

"Chemo," Joelle explained.

"Well. You have a very pretty head."

She laughed again. "Probably thanks to the anti-aging lotion I use."

"It must be working. You don't look a day over eleven."

Giggling, Joelle picked up a cookie. "I like you, Tonya Whatever-your-last-name-is, and not just because you brought food. Though that helps."

Remembering the conversation, Tonya grinned and closed the journal. She should put her initial on the calendar before she forgot, but it didn't seem right.

Today's project hadn't felt like punishment.

Today...well, it kinda felt like Christmas.

> *Dear Journal,*
>
> *Day 7*
>
> *Class party day, and LAST DAY OF SCHOOL! Madison gave me a set of glittery pens. (Doesn't this one write pretty?) I think Mom and Dad forgot about the gift exchange, because they didn't say we couldn't keep what we got. But, just in case, after this entry I'll give the pens away. I'm leaving them and my favorite book (The Lion, the Witch, and the Wardrobe, of course) in the clinic waiting room (where I am now) because the magazines here are BORING.*
>
> *We're here because Brian hurt himself trying to hang Christmas lights for Mr. Fred. He twisted his foot when he jumped off the ladder. I suppose I should be nice and do stuff for him, but he already used up his share of my good deeds. (I think he's reading over my shoulder.) (He just told me he's not.)*
>
> *I can't wait to get home. I'm going to walk Fluffy over to meet Joelle, then invite her family over for supper. Mom said I could. We're going to have cheeseburger soup and homemade bread. Yummy!*

"ALL RIGHT, KIDDOS, THIS IS YOUR FIVE-MINUTE warning," Mom called the next afternoon. "We're leaving to see Great-Grandpa Floyd at one thirty on the dot."

Brian groaned. "Do I have to go?" He exaggerated his hobble as he passed Tonya.

Tonya rolled her eyes. "I'm pretty sure you can have your pick of wheelchairs once we get there. But didn't they say your ankle was fine, just a little bruised?"

"It's a sprain. A light one, but still...a sprain. And it hurts."

"Going to a nursing home is going to make that worse, how?"

He shrugged, cast a glance toward the kitchen, then said, "It kinda makes everything worse."

At the nursing home, the employees had tried to make the place festive. There was a big Christmas tree in the lobby, but the decorations looked as old and brittle as the residents, and the cinnamon-scented plug-ins only added a new layer to the odor that belonged specifically to the nursing home.

Some residents had visitors. Most did not. Some greeted them with a cheerful "Merry Christmas!" Others stared sadly into space.

Brian was right about this place. The sooner they got out of here the better. Great-Grandpa Floyd would understand. Hadn't he tried to escape three times?

Clutching her journal, Tonya filed into the room behind Brian.

"Merry Christmas, Gramps," Mom said.

"Is it Christmas already?" Great-Grandpa turned away from the window and fastened his eyes on Tonya. "You brought elves!"

So began a typical visit. Tonya never knew when Great-Grandpa Floyd was joking or suffering from Old-Timers' Disease, but he sure was entertaining. Today, though, she couldn't stop thinking of the lonely people they'd passed on the way in.

"I have a great idea," Brian whispered as Great-Grandpa dozed off midsentence.

"Remember what happened with your last great idea?" Tonya asked.

"Don't start." He glowered at her. "Do you want to hear it or not?"

"Nope." But she listened anyway.

Dear Journal,

 Day 6

 Today we went caroling. Not around the neighborhood, and not a bunch of us, but it was fun. Me and Brian (Mom tagged along some too) went from room to room at the nursing home and sang all the Christmas songs we could think of. We even did special requests! It made people happy.

It made me happy.

P.S. I don't hate the nursing home anymore.

P.P.S. But it still smells funny.

Dear Journal,

Day 5

I gave away my red hat. The one I spent a month's allowance to buy, just in case I got the coat to match for Christmas.

I'm not getting the coat, so Joelle got my hat. She says she's going to wear it when she comes to church with us tomorrow, but she's afraid she's going to be the only one bald and wearing a hat.

I told her there are lots of bald people at our church. My dad, for starters. She laughed. She laughs a lot. I don't know if I could. If it was me, I mean. As much as my frizzy hair drives me crazy, well...I just don't know if I could. It makes no gifts under the tree this year seem like not such a huge deal anymore.

Kind of.

THE LIGHTS TWINKLED FROM THE EAVES AS THE Rutherford family returned home from the special Sunday evening Christmas program. After their full day, Tonya tucked her feet into fuzzy slippers and collapsed on the couch with hot chocolate and a gingerbread man.

Brian dropped to the floor beside her. "Give me your cookie and I'll dislike you a little less."

"How much less?"

"Eight percent."

"Not worth it." Tonya bit off the leg and chewed. "Mmm. Oven fresh and oh so yummy. You should try one."

"I can't move. My ankle…"

"Yeah, yeah."

"Hey, it could count for the thing."

Tonya worked on the second leg. "What thing?"

"The thing. The calendar."

She nearly dropped her hot chocolate. "I totally forgot." Her stomach went all queasy. "I can't believe I forgot."

"So you'll get me a cookie?"

"Here." Tonya shoved hers at him.

Brian swallowed it in one bite, then grinned. "You know that didn't count, right?"

"Right." Neither did her afternoon walk with Fluffy. But she couldn't think of a thing to do before her bedtime in fifteen minutes. Tonya trudged to the refrigerator and trailed a finger across the calendar to the day's date. Her brow wrinkled as she studied her name written in cursive below Brian's *B*.

Mom bustled into the kitchen, dressed in her nursing clothes. "You need anything before I head out, honey?"

"No, but...did you put my name on here?"

Mom cast a glance at the calendar. "I figured you'd forgotten, so I went ahead and wrote it for you."

"But...I didn't do anything." Tonya's voice came out small. "Today got so busy that I just...forgot."

"Oh, honey." Mom set down her purse and knelt in front of Tonya. "Don't you remember? You set up chairs for the pageant. You wore a hat to help Joelle feel comfortable and introduced her to everyone. You opened the car door for Mrs. Smith. Mrs. Foley called and told me how appreciative she was of you walking her dog for her." Mom wrapped her arms around Tonya. "Those are only the things that *I* know about. I'm guessing, if you thought really hard, you'd come up with some other kindnesses you did just because it was the right thing to do. The fact that you don't remember tells me you've already learned the lesson well. I'm so proud of you."

Tonya sniffed. "Really?"

Her mom gave her one final squeeze. "Really. Now, I've got to run. Sleep well, sweetheart."

Tonya glanced at the calendar and smiled. "I will."

Dear Journal,

Day 3

It snowed today. A lot! We went sledding down Old Calhoun hill. JP from down the road doesn't have a sled, so I let him use mine because I needed to do my project today— shovel the driveway before Dad gets home from work. He always does it for Mom, but nobody does it for him. It took forever! He made it back before I finished, but we had a snowball fight with Brian and JP, and we won! Then we went inside and he drank the coffee I made him. (I think he used some of it to water Mom's plants. I wonder if that helps them grow better.)

Tonya tapped her pen against her chin and glanced through the window. The snow continued to fall, but she felt all marshmallowy inside, remembering how tired and warm his eyes had looked when he'd smiled and thanked her. He worked hard—she might not know exactly what he did in his office, but she *did* know that. Maybe she should look for things to make his life easier more often... even if it didn't count.

THE DAY BEFORE CHRISTMAS EVE, TONYA FELT AS STIFF as the Barbie she wouldn't be getting, with the tension of having only two days left on the project. Two more acts of kindness before Christmas Day, so they *had* to be good. She stayed alert while Mom dragged them around town—delivering presents and buying food—but couldn't come up with anything epic.

Then, just as they pulled in the driveway after their last stop, Mom's cell phone rang its special work ring. Mom closed her eyes, sighed, then answered as she motioned for us to start carrying in the groceries.

"You know we're about to witness a meltdown, right?" Brian asked as he held the door for Tonya.

Had he ever held the door for her? Tonya tried to remember and couldn't. It was nice, but he'd better not think that counted. "Maybe they're just asking her a question."

"Yeah. Like, 'Will you work this shift for me? Because I have things to do, and you're so sweet you won't say no.'"

"Did you just call Mom sweet?"

"No. I just said *they* would think that."

Giggling, Tonya put her bag on the kitchen counter. Brian was right, though. Mom would say yes, and then when she got home she'd clean and cook and be so exhausted when company finally came, she'd probably sleep through the party.

"Hey, Brian. I have an idea."

He gave her a look and started for the door, walking backwards. "Guess what happened last time you had an idea?"

"Have you not forgiven me yet?"

"Have you forgiven me?"

She rolled her eyes. "Yes. I guess. Don't run into the wall."

He caught himself and turned. "I'll have to think about it."

"Running into the wall? Or forgiving me?"

He didn't answer.

Dear Journal,

Day 2

Mom took us on errands today. They took longer than she'd planned, since Mr. and Mrs. Algozzini were in a talkative mood. (Surprise.) (Note the sarcasm.) (Maybe that came across mean. They're actually really funny for old people.)

Long story short, me and Brian got the house ready (my idea!) while Mom worked an extra shift. It's looking pretty sparkly. Dad even helped! It might not be how Mom would have done it, but she'll be grateful we didn't do the cooking instead.

She doesn't get home until super late to-night, but Dad promised to tell us about her reaction. I really hope she likes it.

Tonya twirled her pen between her fingers, then put it back to the paper.

Even though, if I was the mom, I might not have been so mean with the whole present thing, she might have been right. Sort of. At least, I can finally see her point. There's a slight possibility I might have been a little selfish. Even if it was (mostly) Brian's fault.

P.S. I saw Dad watering the plant with my special-made coffee again.

P.P.S. I don't think it's helping.

Dear Journal,
Day 1
Christmas Eve day!!! Grandma Q is flying in. Joelle and half the neighborhood will come to the party tonight. And I already have my initial on the calendar! When I was walking Fluffy, I noticed a delivery man had dropped some packages. I helped pick them up. Then, since it's so very cold and he has to deliver all these presents (none for me, but I'm resigned to my fate), I ran to get him

a coffee refill and cookies. (I'm getting good at the coffee thing. Maybe I should work at Main Street Coffee when I grow up!) Merry Christmas Eve!

P.S. Farewell, 12 Days of Christmas Kindness. I have to admit, it's been kind of fun. (Partly because I finally had somewhere to use my cute stickers.)

Tonya helped in the kitchen that afternoon, then had fun playing with Joelle during the party, but something was missing.

After the party, the family gathered in the living room. Tonya stared up through the Christmas tree lights as Mom and Dad talked about how proud they were of the changes in her and Brian. All the while, Tonya tried to figure out what felt wrong.

Maybe it had been watching Great-Grandpa Floyd as he smiled at all the commotion around him, because then she remembered the sad people in the nursing home without families.

Or maybe it had been looking at Joelle, with her red hat and brown eyes, and realizing that she was not just bald. She was very sick.

Or maybe it had been seeing the pastor drop in, and remembering the orphans she'd learned about in Sunday school.

"All I did was give out a few cookies," she mumbled.

"What was that?" Dad asked.

Tonya hadn't meant to interrupt. But since she had, she sat up and said what she'd been thinking.

Mom gave a soft smile, the one that made Tonya feel extra special. "With your Christmas Countdown project, we wanted you both to notice what was going on around you and become more helpful. But you're right—there are a lot of hurting people out there, and you can't help them all."

"But you still need to do your part." Dad rested his hand on Brian's shoulder. "The things you do matter. They can make you a better person, and even if it's something that seems small, it can be a huge deal to whoever you're helping."

"Your project is over, but we hope you'll keep trying to help the needs around you." Mom beamed at them. "Meanwhile, your father and I have an announcement to make."

"We're going to have a kid brother?" Brian guessed.

Mom looked so shocked Tonya thought maybe Brian was right.

Then Dad laughed so hard he snorted. "No, Brian. It's a little less miraculous than that. In fact, let me show you…" He left, then came back hauling two boxes—one marked Donate, the other, Return.

Brian let out a whoop while Tonya just stared.

"We decided we wanted to give you your gifts anyway. And there might be a few surprises in there too."

"I didn't see that coming," Brian said.

Tonya grinned at her brother as Dad placed the rewrapped packages around the tree. There would be Christmas at the Rutherford home after all.

AFTER EVERYONE HAD GONE TO BED, ELECTRIC candles and strings of lights sent odd shadows flickering over the walls as Tonya tiptoed back to the living room. She couldn't sleep. Every time she closed her eyes, she saw the presents. Mounds of them—more than before. Kneeling by the tree, she found one with her name on it and reached for it, then found the next. Seven gifts in all. Some of them she could tell by the shape what was inside. Others she shook gingerly.

"What are you doing?" someone hissed.

Tonya jerked her head up to find Brian, his face as guilty as hers. "It's not what it looks like."

"Right. This isn't either." He reached for a box with his name on it. "I just needed to see if—"

The chandelier sprang to life, and Dad stood there, arms folded. "What's going on?" Mom stepped up behind him, her face wrinkled as if she were about to cry.

"It appears we were wrong, Ann." Dad's voice was tired. "Kids, go to your rooms. We'll deal with you shortly."

Tonya started to speak, but bit her lip at the silencing look her father shot in her direction. Maybe she should have thought through her actions a little more. For now...she just had to wait.

Mom closed the door to Tonya's room and sat Indian style on the bed, looking Tonya full in the face. "I need to understand what just happened," she said. "You did so well with the project. You seemed to finally get what we were teaching you. Why did you disobey again?"

Tonya hadn't *technically* disobeyed. The standing rule, as she understood it, was no opening presents before permission was given. She hadn't opened them. Not this time.

This probably wasn't the best time to point that out.

"You will not be getting presents," Mom continued, running a hand through her hair. It looked like she'd been doing that a lot. "But we haven't figured out your punishment. I need to know why you disobeyed first."

"I was counting them."

"Why?"

"Remember what you said about it being better to give than to receive?"

Mom nodded.

"I got to thinking." Tonya looked away. "On Sunday, there were still angels left on the tree at church. Seven, I think. I couldn't sleep, because I was thinking about those angels and the seven kids, and that maybe they were good all year long, but they still won't get any presents at all. And I have gifts under the tree that I didn't think I'd be getting and I was okay with it."

Mom let out a weird sound—half laughing-snort, half something else—and Tonya turned back to look at her.

"Mom, I have seven presents under the tree. It might be too late, and they're probably not what those kids wanted, but...do you think we could give my gifts to them?"

In answer, Mom gave Tonya a long hug, rubbing Tonya's hair like she used to do when Tonya was little.

That was probably a yes.

Dear Journal,

Day 0

Merry Christmas! Mom got me up way too early this morning. We ran to the parsonage before she even combed my frizz. We dropped off my gifts, and the pastor's wife promised to see what she could do. Back home, Grandma Q had breakfast ready—cinnamon roll French toast—my favorite! Then we opened presents. I still had a stocking to open, and Mom and Dad liked the presents I bought them at the Christmas store at school. (I wanted to make coffee, but Dad beat me to it while I was out with Mom.) Grandma Q gave me money. Brian opened his presents, but he was missing a few. Most notably, the RipStik. Probably his punishment from snooping last night—he didn't tell me what Dad said to him. Mom has some fun stuff and food—lots of food—planned for the rest of the day. And somewhere, I hope a little girl is opening a box with my red coat.

Brian's hollering at me. Did I ever tell you how annoying he is? I guess that's a brother for you. Gotta go. Merry Christmas.

"Hey, airhead! Are you coming or what?"

Tonya tucked the journal under her pillow and ran for the kitchen. "Sheesh. What do you—?" She skidded to a halt when she found the whole family standing by the back door. "What's going on?"

"I was thinking we should play outside for a while," Brian said. "The sun's shining, the weather's nice..."

It was freezing, and he was crazy. But she knew that already. This was a trick. "Is JP out there ready to ambush me?" She tried to look around him to see outside.

"Would I do that?" Brian asked.

Mom and Dad raised their eyebrows. Tonya nodded. Grandma Q scooted her glasses a little further down her nose.

Brian harrumphed. "He's not out there. Just cooperate for a whole minute, would you?"

Tonya slowly moved forward and slid her coat from a hook by the door. "What do you want to play?"

"Well, the streets are clear, so I thought we could mess around with this." He whipped the red RipStik skateboard out from behind his back, his grin nearly splitting his face.

"But how—?" Tonya tilted her head. "You didn't open—"

"It's yours!" He shoved it into her hands. "Merry Christmas!"

She didn't get it.

"That's what Brian was doing last night," Dad explained. "He was checking to see if he was still getting the RipStik, because he knew how much you wanted one. So he asked us to give it to you instead."

Dear Journal,

I guess that means Brian forgives me all the way. He can be sweet once in a while. Who knew?

But I still say it's all his fault.

Just because.

SECONDHAND MIRACLE

Susan Call

Delectable aromas wafted in from the kitchen, wrapping Henry Pearson in a blanket of warmth and memories as he relaxed in his recliner near the fireplace. The distinct, inviting scent of cinnamon and the tang of crisp Granny Smith apples joined the heady fragrance of the cardamom in his wife's famous pumpkin pie. Their Thanksgiving celebration would be smaller than usual, but Rose had still made all his favorites. Warmed by crackling fire and the scent of pies in the oven, Henry's mind wandered through memories framed in the collection of photographs gracing the mantel.

"Hello? Are you in there?" Rose teased, leaning forward to kiss him on the forehead. "I've been calling for you, you know."

"You have?" Henry shook himself from his reverie and shifted in his chair, turning his attention to her. "I was just looking at our girls, and all the wonderful memories on the mantel. I miss them." He studied her, smiling at the large swatches of flour that randomly adorned her checkered gingham apron. A smudge of white powder lingered on her cheek like a kiss.

"Henry." She knelt next to his recliner. "I think we should do something different this year for Christmas."

He reached out and brushed the flour from her cheek with his thumb. "What are you thinking, dear?"

"What if we spent only twenty dollars on each other this year? We could just let Christmas be about Christmas, without all the 'extra' stuff."

Any other year her request might have surprised Henry. But this year, it made sense. In July they'd downsized from the home they'd shared for over forty years, the house where they had raised their family. Together they thinned out years' worth of "collecting," holding on only to those items they both truly treasured.

Henry recognized the tone of Rose's proposal, having heard it many times over the years. It was the tone that said, "I've been thinking about this for a while." Her heart was in every thought-out word.

"Twenty dollars? Are you sure?" he asked, knowing Rose's mind was already made up.

"Think about it, Henry," Rose said. "We can still find something meaningful for each other. We don't need all the fuss and we definitely don't need more stuff. Don't you agree?"

"Well, I suppose you're right. If that's what you want to do, I can agree to that."

He smiled at her, breathing in the waves of spice from the kitchen. "I bet if the girls could smell your cooking, they'd all be here today."

"I know, honey. I wish they were here too," she said. "At least Beth and the kids will be stopping by for dessert a bit later, and you know they'll all be here for Christmas," she said, rising, then leaning in to give Henry a kiss on the cheek. "I'd better go check on the pies."

HENRY THOUGHT IT SOUNDED SIMPLE ENOUGH. IN FACT, at the time he agreed to Rose's idea, he thought he'd be getting off easier, that somehow finding just one gift would require less shopping. But in the days and weeks that followed, the magnitude of the challenge became evident. Still empty handed, he longed to find something truly special. Never much of a shopper, he'd been taken far out of his comfort zone. His determination over the past two weeks pushed him to brave crowded department stores, bustling shopping malls, and even the quaint shops of their Victorian downtown on numerous occasions. Sales flyers lured him with hopes of securing just the right *something* for Rose. But, despite his noble efforts, success had eluded him. The marathon shopping of the past weeks seemed to prove almost too much for the rugged retired sailor. Confidently he'd leave the house, only to return hours later, feeling defeated.

CHRISTMAS EVE MORNING ARRIVED BEFORE HE WAS ready, and still he had no idea what meaningful gift to give his beloved wife. He knew the mall would be open at some ridiculously early hour, but he couldn't quite bring himself to go there. And besides, what would he see there that he hadn't already seen? The time had come to switch it up—to find a new strategy. After all, he was out of time.

There was one more store he hoped to search, a new secondhand store at the far end of town. He'd looked everywhere else. Maybe, just maybe, he'd have better luck there.

After having his morning coffee, clearing the driveway and sidewalk of the thick blanket of snow that had fallen overnight, and having lunch with Rose, he climbed into his car, determined to find *something* that would delight his wife.

"Lord," Henry bowed his head and whispered, "please help me find something that will bless Rose this Christmas." It was already one o'clock. If he hurried, he could make it back in time to attend the early Christmas Eve service with his wife. He glanced at his watch again, then added, "Lord, I could use a miracle today."

THE SECONDHAND SHOP WAS NOT PROMISING, LOOKING more like a flea market than anything else. But the eleventh hour had arrived, and he'd run out of options. *Here goes,* he thought. His eyes glanced around the crowded shop, which was almost bursting at the seams with "gently used" goods. Large televisions and stereos lined one wall, crowding the walkway in front of them. Clothing hung on racks in the back corner, and appliances lined the opposite wall. Near the front of the store, several guitars hung above a drum set, and Henry chuckled as his eyes caught a glimpse of a tuba sitting next to the drums. *Probably not for Rose,* he thought.

Reminding himself of his twenty-dollar budget, he squared his shoulders and quickly assessed the options, zeroing in on a glass case across from the musical instruments. He cleared his throat, gaining the attention of a bored-looking young store clerk.

"Could I see this tray?" Henry asked, pointing to the small collection of knick-knacks in the glass display case.

"Sure." The clerk reached into his pocket to pull out an oversized ring filled with keys, then unlocked the case and pulled out the top tray. Feeling a surge of optimism, Henry sifted methodically through the eclectic assortment. His large hand confidently scooped up several items and sorted out the pieces. A green frog-shaped broach with red eyes stared back at him balefully. Henry shifted the items to reveal a small brown pair of tiger-eye cuff links previously hiding beneath the frog. *Nope,* Henry thought as he focused on a gray elephant-shaped lapel pin, chipped and missing half of its paint.

Henry emptied his hand and scooped up a new batch of trinkets. He sorted through the items, lifting out an old costume-jewelry ring with an empty socket for a bauble that was now long gone, and a ring of assorted old keys. He emptied his hand still again, feeling his hope fade with each failed attempt.

As he searched, Rose's words haunted him. *"We just don't need more stuff."* He knew whatever he found needed to be special. Looking at the pile, he felt certain they had all been treasures once to someone. Could there be something hiding here that could be a treasure for Rose? *Please, Lord*, Henry prayed silently. He stirred the tray with his fingers, combing through the collection, uncovering new knickknacks hiding beneath the first layer. With each unique and interesting item his hand touched, his heart sank a bit lower. Nothing seemed *right*. Doubt began to echo in his mind. *I'm never going to find something worthwhile for less than twenty dollars.*

"Do you need help finding something, sir?" the clerk asked, interrupting Henry's drifting thoughts.

"No," Henry said, startled. "No...I'm not really sure what I'm looking for." All he knew was, he'd know exactly what *it* was when he found it.

"Do you have another tray that I could look through?" Henry asked.

"Sure," the clerk sighed, as if the request required more effort than he hoped to expend. The clerk snatched up the first tray, shook it quickly so the items could settle, and returned it. Then he reached down to a lower, partially obscured shelf and pulled out a smaller tray of miscellaneous odds and ends. He set the tray on the counter in front of Henry with a clatter. "If you need anything else, let me know." He retreated to the back of the counter, where he picked up his cell phone and began tapping on the screen.

Henry's eyes slowly scanned the new tray. *This looks just like the last batch*, he thought. His head dropped as he let out a sigh. Suddenly, he remembered his prayer for a small miracle earlier that morning. Over the years of their marriage, they had been blessed by God's faithfulness. Today's prayer seemed so insignificant after all of their challenges through the years. Henry and Rose had begun their marriage separated by oceans. They witnessed the miracle of birth with their daughters and, more recently, had successfully fought Rose's serious bout with cancer. Now he had one simple heartfelt but seemingly insignificant request. *Lord, this would be a really good time. I need Your help,* Henry prayed as his thought shifted back to the task at hand.

His eyes lifted, focusing on the tray once again. *Here goes,* he thought, slowly scooping up a few items. He sifted out a ladybug charm and an oversized scratched cameo pin, and then his eyes stopped to focus on a small pendant on a thin silver chain.

The front of the circle-shaped charm had a now-faded pink rose visible through the scratches in the surface. Henry cracked a faint smile as he discarded all of the other baubles in his hand, holding on to the charm alone. Leaning in, he inspected the find more closely. Then slowly he turned it over to reveal the back.

Etched into the metal finish were four unusual letters: *WAML*.

Henry's heart nearly stopped. He ran his forefinger across the letters, loosely tracing each letter. He exhaled deeply before an affectionate smile bloomed and tears welled in his steel-blue eyes. The old sailor didn't often show emotion, but suddenly he couldn't contain himself. He recognized the worn pendant with the faded rose and the hand-carved letters that adorned it. In fact, he had carefully carved those wobbly letters on the back himself.

For years Rose kept it in a shallow clay saucer on her dresser. One day, it was gone. Henry speculated it had been pocketed by an unscrupulous contractor during their home renovation. But they never quite knew for certain what became of it—was it stolen, or simply lost?

Henry's fingers curled around the charm, almost as to give it an embrace. *How did it come to be here?* he wondered as his smile grew. "How?" he whispered as he let out a long, slow exhale, making room to breathe in every last facet of this moment. He knew Rose would want him to report all the details.

"How much—?" His voice cracked as he attempted to speak. He cleared his throat, paused, and asked again, the second time more firmly. "How much for this one?"

"Sir, that one with the chain..." The clerk's voice trailed off as he looked down at the price sheet for the items in the tray. "That one is $17.95, plus tax."

A miracle! Henry thought, and later, as he drove home with his treasure, he realized, *No, two miracles.* Finding it, and the fact that, even after tax, it still squeaked in under the twenty-dollar limit. After weeks of struggling with what had become a daunting challenge, Henry was bursting with joy. Now the difficulty he'd had finding the perfect gift paled in comparison to keeping it a secret—even if Christmas was only a day away.

CHRISTMAS MORNING ARRIVED NOT A MOMENT TOO soon for Henry. Outside, a magical fresh dusting of snow again coated the landscape. Henry gladly put a few logs in the fireplace, and planned to keep the room aglow as his contribution to the family gathering.

"Merry Christmas!" Sarah called, opening the back door and stomping snow from her boots. Sarah's eight-year-old son, George, followed in her wake. "We made it! Wow. Something smells amazing!"

"You know your mother's been cooking up a storm in the kitchen." Henry hugged them and took their coats. "Merry Christmas, sweetheart. It's good to have you home."

"It's great to be home! Oh, Lisa's right behind us. Did Beth and her family make it yet?" Sarah asked.

"They'll be here in just a few minutes, and then the whole gang will be here," Rose said, coming to join them in the hallway. "Merry Christmas, honey." She bent down to give George a hug. "Your timing is perfect. Dinner's just about ready. Sarah, can you help your dad put water on the table? He keeps getting distracted."

A short while later, Henry and Rose's quiet home was filled with joyful sounds of conversation, laughter, and clinking forks as they enjoyed her pies.

"I can't eat another bite! Everything was great, Mom," Beth said.

Once the table was cleared and the dishes done, the family gathered in the living room. "Presents!" one of the grandkids squealed.

"You'll have to take turns getting them from under the tree," Rose said, pointing to the beautifully wrapped packages. One by one, the gifts were handed out and opened until the space beneath the tree was almost bare.

"Last one!" George announced.

"It's for you, Dad, from Mom," Sarah said, inspecting the tag on the large gift. "Here you go." She handed the package to Henry.

"Well, let's see what we have here," he said, slowly slipping his finger methodically beneath each piece of tape. When he released the last piece of tape, the paper gently slid to the floor.

"Open it already, Dad!" Lisa said. "You're torturing us!"

Henry lifted the lid off the big box, revealing a navy-blue-and-cream-colored checkerboard afghan.

"I made that, dear," Rose said with a smile.

Henry reached in the box and scooped out the blanket, unfolding its soft warmth across his lap. He knew Rose had crocheted it with love. "It's beautiful, Rose. Thank you."

"I was so careful to work on it while you were busy so I didn't spoil the surprise," Rose said.

Henry's smile grew. He'd certainly given her ample time with his mostly fruitless shopping expeditions. "It's perfect."

"That's it," Sarah said, returning to her seat. "There aren't any more."

Henry pulled himself out of his recliner and lovingly folded his afghan, placing it over the arm of his chair. "I want to share a story with you, if you'll indulge an old man." His eyes twinkled as he looked at each one of those gathered in the cozy living room. "Having all of you here with us has made me a little nostalgic."

"Well, don't keep us in suspense, Henry," Rose teased him. "Tell us your story."

"Yeah, Poppop, tell us," George chimed in.

Henry moved to the middle of the room, tapped his cane on the wooden floor, and began transporting his family back in time sixty years earlier, to Henry and Rose's first Christmas as a couple. Newly engaged, Henry and Rose were halfway across the country from each other: Henry at Great Lakes Naval Base completing boot camp, Rose busy with college in Philadelphia to pursue her dream of becoming a nurse.

"This was before cell phones, texting, and unlimited long-distance calling," Henry explained to his incredulous grandchildren. "Your grandma and I couldn't afford to talk to each other on the phone." Instead, he told them, the two often wrote letters that took up to a week to be delivered. It was less than ideal, but they both knew it was only temporary.

AFTER WEEKS OF EXHAUSTING DRILLS AND INTENSE technical training, Henry was thrilled to graduate from boot camp, though unsure what the future would bring. Soon his new home would be the naval base in Newport, Rhode Island. Once there, his unit would quickly deploy to the Mediterranean for several months, unfortunately increasing the physical distance between him and Rose.

Several days before the journey to his new base, Henry managed to secure a pass for a one-day leave. The distance from home, and especially from Rose, tugged at his heart. Suddenly the reality of life out at sea, and the inability to talk with her, weighed heavily. He desperately hoped to find a small Christmas present for her on his day off, something that would let her know how much he loved her, even though they were far apart. Unsure how he could even get the gift to her, he planned to buy something that could easily be mailed if need be. Henry was glad to have the company of another sailor, Paul, while he shopped. Paul too was looking for a gift for his girlfriend back home.

The two wandered into a shop near the naval base. "What about this for Rose?" Paul asked, pointing to a nice blue-and-white cardigan hanging just inside the door.

"That might be too bulky to mail," Henry answered.

"You're probably right," Paul agreed. Both Henry and Paul were quick to realize the challenge of finding something small, light, easy to mail, and personal. It seemed like quite a tall order in such limited time.

"I think I'll get one of these," Paul said, pointing to a rack of silk scarves and seeming thrilled by his sudden success. "Now I just have to figure out which one."

Henry stepped up to the glass case next to the register. His eyes scanned the shelves of necklaces, earrings, bracelets, and other baubles. On the bottom shelf, a silver necklace with a charm caught his eye.

"Could I see this one?" he asked the bubbly store clerk.

"Of course." She giggled. "You must be shopping for someone special." She retrieved the necklace from the case and handed it to Henry. He inspected the beautiful pink rose on the front of the charm.

"Rose will love this. It's perfect," he said, handing it back to the cashier so she could ring it up.

After returning to base, Henry wanted to add a finishing touch to his gift. He took up Paul's offer to use a tool in a repair shop on base where he worked. Henry had only used a Dremel engraving tool a few times before, but he wanted to do the etching himself. On the back of the charm, he carefully carved four letters: *WAML*. Rose would know exactly what it meant.

Only two short days later, Henry's unit received their orders. They'd be heading out by train to their new home base in Rhode Island. Henry knew this could be his chance. If he could get word to Rose, maybe, just maybe, she could meet him when his train passed through the station near her college.

The next day, Henry's unit boarded their buses to start their journey. Once at the train station, Henry wasted no time finding a station attendant. There simply wouldn't be time to search for a pay phone, and he didn't have the change it would require.

"I need to make a phone call. It's really urgent," he said as he pulled out several dollars from his pocket and slipped it to the attendant. By today's standards it wasn't much money, but it was a sacrifice for Henry on his meager income at the time. But it was worth it.

"Right this way, sir," the porter said, discreetly pocketing the cash. He showed Henry to a phone in the corner of the ticket office.

The call would be a long shot. Rose's dormitory had only a few shared phones for the students to use. Calling didn't necessarily mean he would reach her, or even get a message to her. But he knew it was worth every bit of the pay he had given just for the chance. Henry dropped his large duffel bag at his feet, and his hand shook with excitement as he began to dial.

Ring, ring, he heard on the other end of the phone.

A female voice answered. "Hello? May I help you?"

"Is that you, Rose?"

"Henry!" Rose exclaimed. "Is everything okay?"

"Yes. Yes, everything is fine. Rose, I only have a minute. Our train is already pulling in. They're sending us up to Newport, and we'll likely be headed out to sea soon." He cradled the phone close to his ear, as though it might bring her a little bit closer. "We'll be passing through the Thirtieth Street Station on the way to the base. Is there any way you could meet our train?"

"You're c-coming here?" Rose stammered. "Yes, yes, of course I'll go to the station! I miss you, Henry!"

"Miss you too, Rose. You'll need to check with the station to find out when we're passing through. I've got to go. Love you." With that, Henry placed the phone on the receiver and returned his large military-issued duffel bag to his shoulder. He dashed to the train, joining the other sailors already on board just in time.

With a loud "All aboard!" the conductor's voice boomed through the station. The train's loud whistle announced their departure, and the steady clank of rails soon became a constant melody that accompanied the train over the miles.

A draft from the outside winter air whistled through the train, breaking Henry's wandering thoughts. Anxious to see Rose, he found his mind racing far ahead of the train. It was hard to believe in just a few hours, they could exchange a quick embrace. The burst of cool air whipped past Henry, replacing his warm thoughts with a chill. He buttoned up his wool sailor coat and sank into his window seat. Outside the window, the small towns that dotted the sparse landscape provided little distraction to help the time pass. Occasionally Henry closed his eyes, hoping for even a brief nap. But each time he did, he woke up anxious that he had slept through the stop in Philadelphia.

It was near dinnertime when the train finally approached the Thirtieth Street Station. The long journey had seemed even longer accompanied by the anticipation of seeing Rose. Henry carefully walked back to the rear of his train car to wait. Standing next to the luggage compartment, he could look out the larger windows and watch his train's progress. With a few jerky motions, the train switched tracks and pulled into the station. Henry stepped out of the rear door, hanging on to the railings as he leaned forward, scanning the crowd on the platform as the train rolled to a stop.

The sailors had been discouraged from leaving the train at any of the scheduled stops. Still, he hoped that he could quickly slip off and back onto the train. However, that could only be possible if she just happened to be near his railcar on the platform. He prayed and tried to remain optimistic, hoping for enough time to give her a loving embrace and surprise her with the present tucked carefully in his pocket.

His heart raced as he scanned the crowd. He knew how precious little time they'd have together. Nervously, he reached into his coat pocket with his right hand. *It's still there,* he thought, reassured by the confirmation. With the minutes passing quickly by, Henry still saw no sign of Rose amid the holiday travelers. The prospect of spending any real time with her was rapidly diminishing.

The densely crowded platform made searching for Rose difficult. Henry craned forward frantically. *She must be here somewhere*, he thought, determined to find her.

As his eyes anxiously panned the crowd, a second train pulled into the station, stopping on the opposite side of the same platform. Travelers swarmed off the train, creating even more chaos in the busy station.

"All aboard!" the conductor yelled loudly. With a slight jerk, the train wheels slowly slipped into motion. A sense of urgency rushed over Henry as his eyes quickly panned the crowd one last time.

On the far side of the platform, a white cap caught his attention in the sea of bundled travelers. Rose! Standing on her toes, in her white nurse's uniform and cap, even from the distance, Henry could see panic on her face.

"There, there she is! Rose!" he yelled. "Rose!" He jumped and waved his arms from the back of the train, catching her attention.

"Henry!" she yelled, waving in return.

The train's momentum beginning to grow, Henry reached into his pocket. He knew he only had one chance. He exhaled, leaned back, and tossed the surprise gift in Rose's direction.

Almost as if in slow motion, the present spiraled through the air in a dramatic arc, then dropped into the hands of someone standing near Rose. The small crowd of people converged on her and let out a thunderous cheer as they recognized the romance unfolding in the scene. Rose waved back to Henry until his train pulled out of the station and disappeared from his view.

THE HUSH THAT SWEPT OVER THE ROOM WHEN HENRY began his story lingered long after he finished. It was Henry who broke the silence. "You could say that was our first Christmas together—well, almost together," he amended with a smile, stepping back to relinquish the floor.

"Wait!" Sarah protested. "What happened next? You can't end your story there!"

"Your mom will have to tell you," Henry said with a sly smile. "She was the one in the station."

Rose took up the story. "I was on the platform, shaking, convinced that I had missed him. And then, then I saw your dad standing at the back of the train, waving at me. When he threw the package, everyone started to cheer." She smiled at the memory. "A stranger standing near me said, 'I believe this is yours,' and handed me the small package your dad threw."

Rose looked around the room and continued. "I carefully unwrapped the present. Inside was a beautiful charm with a pink rose on the front. When I flipped it over, I immediately noticed the inscription on it."

Rose's eyes misted. "It said *WAML*." She leaned forward in her chair and looked over at Henry. "It means 'With all my love.' I remember looking down the track toward where his train disappeared and whispering, 'I love you too, Henry, with all my love.'"

"Aww, that is so sweet," Lisa said.

"It's like a scene out of a movie," Sarah added. "Mom, I can't believe you never told us that story!"

Rose smiled. "It happened long before you were born. I guess when you were older it just never came up. You know, your father might be a tough sailor, but he's always been a hopeless romantic.

"Oh, I wish you could have seen the crowd on the platform," she continued. "They cheered and cheered. You would have thought we were famous."

"So that's where *WAML* came from!" Beth exclaimed. For years, her parents had often signed cards to each other with those four odd letters.

"Oh, I almost forgot. There's one present left over here," Henry said. With a flourish, he reached to the back of the Christmas tree and pulled out a small package with a pink bow. "It's for you," he said, looking at Rose across the room from where he stood. With a slow swing of his arm, the gift lofted into the air, arcing first up, and then down, landing in George's lap, directly next to Rose.

"You missed her, Poppop," George said.

Henry just grinned.

"Here, Nana," George said, handing the present to his grandmother. "I believe this one is yours."

Rose neatly untied the ribbon and gently pulled the tape off each end, then tore the paper open to reveal a small box. She slowly lifted open the lid and fixed her eyes on the gift inside, a small scratched pendant with a light-pink painted rose. She gasped and turned the charm over. Her eyes focused on the four letters etched on the back.

"Henry," she whispered as she looked up at him with tears in her eyes, "how on earth...?"

"Merry Christmas, Rose," Henry replied, "with all my love."

RING OF KINDNESS

Sarah Forgrave

*T*he party had all the classic hallmarks of Christmas—"Joy to the World" playing on the speakers, the scent of cinnamon swirling in the air, and a dessert table that threatened to add five pounds to a person at a mere glance.

Taryn Richards stood alone in a corner of the Cincinnati megachurch's sprawling foyer, watching as dozens of church employees and their spouses mingled and laughed, while she clutched her plate of uneaten food and blinked back tears. Everything in her wanted to go home and curl up with her Yorkie, Samson, to escape memories of meeting her husband as a newcomer to the staff Christmas party two years before.

A wave of grief swirled through her, and she headed toward the ladies' room. Why had she thought it was a good idea to come tonight?

She unloaded her plate in the trash and ducked into the restroom, where the silence was broken only by the buzz of fluorescent lights. The sound pecked against her frayed emotions. She massaged her temples and glanced in the mirror, taking in the tired lines under her eyes.

Whether she liked it or not, this was her life now. Life as a twenty-eight-year-old widow.

The bathroom door swung open, and the nursery director entered. Resisting the urge to take refuge in a stall, Taryn straightened and smiled. "Hi, Joyce."

The woman came to the mirror and gave Taryn a look of understanding, her silver hair and the crinkles near her eyes reminding Taryn of Mrs. Claus. "Did you need a break from the holiday cheer?"

Taryn nodded, letting Joyce's southern twang ripple across her shoulders and ease her tension. Even though she didn't know Joyce well, the church staff knew Taryn and Michael's story. Knew that a brain tumor had ripped Michael from this world four months into their marriage, leaving Taryn behind with a shattered heart.

Joyce's features softened. "I remember feeling the same way after my husband died." With a gentle pat to Taryn's arm, she said, "It'll get better, I promise."

The futility of it all threatened to swallow Taryn, and her thoughts slipped past her lips in a quiet plea. "When? When will it get better?"

Wisdom filled Joyce's gaze as she shook her head. "Life never moves at the pace we want. Just keep putting one foot in front of the other." Her mouth curved. "One of my favorite verses in Psalms says, 'Though you have made me see troubles, many and bitter, you will restore my life again; from the depths of the earth you will again bring me up.'" She gave Taryn a knowing glance. "God will do the work. Your job is to stay close to Him and listen."

Taryn crossed her arms to ward off a sudden chill. How could she hear God's voice if He'd chosen to remain silent? Not wanting to dismiss the older woman's advice, she nodded. "I'll try."

"That's all God asks." Joyce's sweet voice pressed on. "I'm praying for you. Let me know if there's anything I can do."

"Thanks." Taryn's throat clamped shut, and she finished in the restroom and ducked out behind Joyce. The party continued in full swing, but Taryn couldn't bring herself to go back. Sticking to the perimeter of the foyer, she made a beeline for the exit, stopping to get her coat on the way.

Joyce waved good-bye from across the room, and the motherly concern in her eyes filled Taryn with a longing to see her parents. But no matter how much she craved their presence, they were thousands of miles away, serving as missionaries in Uganda, with no travel funds to visit their only child for Christmas.

Loneliness pressed into her spine, but she shook it off. With a brief glance behind her, she zipped up her coat, escaped the church foyer, and walked outside to her vintage Jeep Cherokee.

AS SHE DROVE INTO HER NEIGHBORHOOD, CHRISTMAS lights twinkled on the small bungalows, and the snow-covered lawns boasted figurines of everything from Santa Claus to baby Jesus to Frosty the Snowman. She kept her gaze on the road until she pulled into the driveway of her two-bedroom home and parked in the carport. When she entered the utility room, Samson's paws pitter-pattered toward her, and the little dog greeted her with a jump on her legs and a playful yip.

"Hey, buddy. Anything exciting happen while I was gone?" She bent down and rubbed his fur, smiling when his slick tongue tickled her fingers. Samson's tail wiggled as he ignored Taryn's question and licked her left hand. He stopped at her ring finger and lifted his head, looking at her with a tilt of his ears as if asking what'd happened to her wedding ring.

"I know. I wish I knew where it was too."

If only she'd gotten the ring resized as soon as she and Michael got back from their honeymoon a year ago—if only she'd known its loose fit would come back to haunt her. But she'd been focused on enjoying their first Christmas as husband and wife. And then one night after Christmas, she discovered it had slipped off her finger without her knowing.

Countless searches later, she'd resigned herself to the fact that it was gone forever.

The dark house pressed in on her, and she stepped into the kitchen and flipped on the lights. She found herself scanning the perimeter of the linoleum, as she'd done a hundred times in her search for the ring, yearning for a sparkle or shimmer to reveal its whereabouts. But the only thing that winked at her was a dust bunny begging for a broom.

Suppressing a sigh, she headed to the living room and settled in the corner armchair where her Christmas tree would be—if she'd put it up this year. Samson soon snuggled up with her, and she spent the next hour flipping through TV channels, skipping past sappy Hallmark movies, network holiday specials, and *A Christmas Story* reruns until she gave up altogether.

As she turned off the TV, Joyce's words from earlier pulsed through her mind. *"God will do the work. Your job is to stay close to Him and listen."*

Would God ever restore her as He'd promised in the Psalm? She understood the part about being in the depths of the earth—understood how it felt to be a shell of a person, with nothing left but a dry, cracked skeleton.

Her Bible sat on the coffee table, beckoning, and she reached for it and leafed through the pages, unsure of what she sought. All she knew was she had to find a way to move forward, to trust that God would breathe life into her.

Otherwise, what else did she have to live for?

The grocery store was blessedly quiet as Taryn pushed her cart through the aisles after work on Tuesday. Her weekend had been filled with manning the missions kiosk at the church's five services and then reading her Bible in snatches between catnaps, but she was no closer to feeling restored than she'd felt after the staff Christmas party.

Now her pantry supply was sparse and Samson's food was almost out, which meant she had to brave civilization and put her meager checking account to the test.

A jazzy rendition of "Winter Wonderland" played softly on the store's speakers as she grabbed a box of raisin bran and set it in her cart, mentally adding the price to the other items in her stash. Dog food would push the limits of her budget, but she should be all right.

When she reached the only open checkout lane fifteen minutes later, Taryn unloaded the food from her cart and onto the conveyer belt. After the last item had been scanned, the tired-looking cashier stated the total in a monotone voice. "Seventy-nine dollars and forty cents."

Taryn's pulse blipped. "How much?"

The cashier repeated the number, impatience edging into her expression.

A flush of heat raced up Taryn's neck and singed her cheeks. She had put aside her credit cards after seeing their balances creep upward, and the bills in her purse couldn't cover the total. How had she ended up fifteen dollars over? Had she remembered to add the dog food when she put it in the cart? Or maybe she'd misread some of the price tags on the shelves. "I'm sorry, I must've miscalculated. Can I take something off?"

The cashier huffed and rolled her eyes toward Taryn's cart loaded with grocery bags. "Pull out what you don't want. I'll have to get a manager to do a void."

Taryn reached for the first sack and took inventory. Milk, deli meat, cheese. She could always make lunch sandwiches with just the meat—

A throat cleared behind her, and the sound pulled her upright.

"Excuse me, miss." The voice belonged to an elderly man in line behind her. Dark age spots dotted his skin, and tufts of white hair poked out from under his plaid ivy cap. He shuffled toward Taryn and held out his hand. "This is for you."

Taryn glanced down with a start when she saw four twenties splayed out like a fan in his quivering fingers. "Oh no, I couldn't take it."

He pressed the money closer, and the corners of his mouth lifted. "I insist. A nice young lady visited me yesterday and brought a plate of Christmas cookies. Told me to pass the kindness on." He pulled a white card from the stack of bills and handed it to Taryn. "She gave me this."

Taryn took the card and read its words.

> *You've just been given a random act of kindness.*
> *Pass the blessing on to a stranger, along with this card.*
> *"No act of kindness, no matter how small, is ever*
> *wasted."—Aesop*

"So you see"—the man's voice danced with merriment—"if you turn me down, you'll take away my chance to pass along the blessing." He kept his hand outstretched.

How could she accept his gift? Eighty dollars? It was too much.

The cashier coughed and raised a brow as she glanced pointedly at the growing line of customers behind them. "Ma'am?"

Before Taryn could stop him, the man pressed the bills into her palm, held fast to her hand, and reached it toward the cashier. "She's going to accept my gift and be on her way."

Emotion pricked her eyes, but she blinked and smiled at the stranger. "Thank you. If there's any way I can repay…"

He shook his head. "Just do what the card says and pass it on." He turned to his cart and busied himself transferring items to the belt.

Heart in her throat, she took her receipt from the cashier, thanked the man again when he insisted she keep the change, and exited the store to the parking lot. Her mind replayed the scenario, and she shook her head at the craziness of this random act of kindness.

And now she'd been charged with passing it on.

The frigid air numbed her fingers as she gripped the cart handle, guilt intertwining with her disbelief. After almost a year of being on the receiving end of prayers, sympathy cards, and meals, did she even know how to see the needs of others anymore? Sure, her job was others-focused with the mission trips she coordinated for the church, but somewhere along the way it had become just a job.

The jangle of a bell filled her ears, and she glanced at the woman standing by a Salvation Army bucket near the store's exit. Taryn slowed her steps and dropped her benefactor's change into the bucket with a hollow clatter. Did that qualify as her act of kindness?

No, it needed to be something bigger. Something unexpected.

As she walked to her SUV, her gaze strayed to the other customers walking to and from the store, her mind suddenly viewing them differently. Did any of them need help?

Everyone appeared to be going about their business, so she loaded her groceries in her vehicle and drove home to a warm greeting from Samson.

Samson bounded into the kitchen to his near-empty food bowl, looking at Taryn eagerly. "I know, I know. All you care about is your stomach." She opened Samson's food and topped off his bowl.

As he munched away, she emptied the rest of the grocery sacks, pulling the receipt from the last bag and adding it to a pile of papers on the counter.

At the top of the stack, a flyer peeked out from her church bulletin—a reminder about the Christmas event their church was hosting this Saturday for under-resourced families. Since the event wasn't under her umbrella of ministry, Taryn had planned to sit it out.

But what if this was her chance to pass along the kindness card the man had given her? No, she thought.

In order to count as a "random act of kindness," didn't it have to be something unique and thoughtful?

Leaving the flyer in its place, she pulled a mug from the cabinet, filled it with water, and heated it in the microwave. She withdrew a packet of hot cocoa from her pantry and mixed it into the mug, then sat down with it in her corner chair. The pastor had said they needed more hosts—people willing to spend the day with the families at the church, walking them through the process of going to the food pantry and helping them choose Christmas gifts for their kids.

Taryn's thumb massaged her empty ring finger as she conjured up excuses to avoid the event. What would she, as a widow, have to offer these families? What would she say? Surely other people had already stepped up and volunteered. She needed to save her energy for working at the weekend services.

Samson left his food bowl and jumped in her lap, his warm body easing the chill in her legs. Her mind went back to the countless acts of service people had given her this past year, and conviction burned inside. She drank another sip of cocoa and snuggled Samson close. "What do you think? Should I do it?"

His mouth opened in a wide yawn, and he rested his chin on his paws, settling in for a nap and leaving the decision to her.

At this point, she had two choices—sit at home on Saturday morning, drowning in her pain like she'd done for the past eight months, or get out of the house and look for a chance to pass the kindness card to someone else.

Before she could back out, she grabbed her phone from the table and sent an e-mail to the coordinators of the Christmas event, letting them know she would volunteer. With a deep exhale, she set down her phone and stroked Samson's fur. "Well, buddy, looks like you're hanging out here by yourself on Saturday."

The warm aroma of coffee greeted Taryn when she arrived at the church for her volunteer duties Saturday morning. The outreach team scurried around, making sure supplies were set up and volunteers were ready to minister to the two hundred families who'd registered for the event.

The morning would start with breakfast, then the kids would go off to the children's area for special activities while the parents selected gifts from the thousands of toy donations. Each family would also receive a box of clothing and stop by the food pantry, where they would receive three bags of groceries.

Taryn couldn't help but think of the gift that had been added to her pantry earlier this week, thanks to the elderly man's generosity.

As she crossed the foyer to the volunteer sign-in area, she felt in her coat pocket for the kindness card and determined to keep her eyes open for opportunities. No wallowing in sadness today. This was about meeting others' needs—something she'd needed to do for far too long.

After going through a brief orientation with the other hosts, she headed to the worship center, which had been converted into a large banquet hall. Round tables were decked out with tablecloths and candle centerpieces marked with numbers. She found her assigned table and sat in a chair, waiting for her family's arrival.

Nerves zipped through her stomach and dried her mouth. What would her family be like? She'd only been given the mother's name—Shawna Anderson. Would she be easy to talk to, or would they struggle to make conversation?

If only Michael were here. Normally he would've been the one to jump at an opportunity like this, his outgoing personality making him a natural fit for the church's sports ministry and a perfect counterbalance to Taryn's shyness.

She rubbed the empty spot on her ring finger and forced her thoughts on the moment. *Lord, keep me focused today.*

A rustle of movement drew near, and an ebony-skinned woman dropped into the seat next to Taryn, bringing the scent of tropical flowers with her. She glanced at the table number and exhaled a winded breath. "Are we in the right place?"

Taryn shoved down her anxiety and smiled. "Are you Shawna?"

The woman nodded, cranberry-red ringlets dancing around her friendly face. "What's your name?"

"Taryn. I'm your host, so I'll be walking you through the process today."

"That's wonderful. God bless you for being here." Shawna motioned to the children huddling at the edge of the table. "Come on, kids, have a seat."

The four children sat down, their heads making stair steps of height. The oldest boy appeared to be in middle school, the two girls elementary age, and the youngest boy a wiggly, bright-eyed preschooler. "Looks like you have your hands full."

Shawna chuckled. "That's the truth. Being a single mom isn't easy, but I wouldn't trade them for anything."

After quick introductions, the kids discovered the coloring pages and crayons in the middle of the table and busied themselves while Shawna barreled ahead, carrying the conversation. "This opportunity is such a blessing. Our house burned down two months ago, so I didn't think we'd be able to have Christmas this year."

They'd lost their house two months before Christmas? Taryn pressed her lips together. "I'm sorry."

Shawna's features smoothed and she shook her head. "It's all right. All that matters is the Lord spared my babies. Everything else is just stuff."

An ache settled behind Taryn's rib cage as memories with Michael resurfaced—all the times they'd shared their love of the outdoors and hiked through state parks, then the autumn hike when he got down on one knee and put a sparkling diamond on her finger. Money had been tight when they got married, with both of them working for a nonprofit while saving for a down payment on their house, so they'd forgone purchasing a wedding band until a later anniversary. When she'd lost her only ring after their honeymoon, Michael had been so calm, assuring her it would show up someday, reminding her that a piece of jewelry didn't define them.

"Do you have any kids?" Shawna asked, pulling Taryn from her thoughts. Other families had started to file toward the food line, but Shawna stayed in place and waited for Taryn's answer.

She shook her head. "Just a Yorkie named Samson." Should she mention the fact that she'd been married? That she'd always wanted a houseful of kids? She twined her fingers in her lap and looked down with a swallow. "My husband passed away eight months ago."

"Oh, honey," Shawna crooned. "And here you are helping others. The Lord will honor your generosity, just wait and see."

A dry laugh threatened to escape, but Shawna's youngest son pulled his mom's attention from Taryn with a tug on her sleeve. "Can we get our food now?"

"Sure, sweetie." Shawna took his hand and stood, grinning at Taryn as she ushered her kids toward the food line. "Duty calls."

Taryn went to the line with her and helped the kids load their plates with eggs, sausage, muffins, and fruit. As she waited for the line to move, she took in the scene around her.

More than a thousand people filled the room, laughter and chatter blending with the accompaniment of acoustic guitar. Farther up in line, Taryn spotted Joyce standing with her assigned family. She wore a red velvet hat over her silver hair, her Mrs. Claus–like aura garnering stares of awe from the children around her. A twinkle glimmered in her eyes as she looked back and gave Taryn an approving nod.

Taryn warmed at the realization she was doing what Joyce had advised a week ago—putting one foot in front of the other and leaving the rest up to God.

Soon the line moved, and they returned to their table. Taryn helped the youngest boy with his food, and as she cut his sausage into bite-sized pieces, she scrambled for a way to get him talking. "What's your favorite thing about Christmas?"

His gaze grew serious, and earnestness filled his voice. "Our Christmas tree got burned down by a fire, but Mommy says we don't need one this year."

Taryn paused, her plastic knife hovering midair as their situation weighed down on her. Even though she couldn't bring herself to get out her Christmas decorations, every child needed a tree to admire, to awaken their imagination.

"It's all right, Devon," Shawna said. "As long as we have each other, we'll have a happy Christmas, won't we?"

His head bobbed in a melancholy nod, and one of his sisters piped up from across the table, a heavy sigh preceding her words. "But I lost my special angel ornament. I can't have Christmas without my angel."

Taryn's mind rewound to her first and only Christmas with Michael, when he'd stretched to his tallest height to put her frilly white angel on top of the tree. He'd teased her about it not being manly enough, but he'd put it up anyway.

Now it collected dust in a box with all her other decorations.

"I have an angel you can use. And a tree." The offer rushed from her mouth before she could think it through.

"Oh no, you don't have to do that," Shawna said. "We'll be fine."

Taryn noted the way the children's posture had straightened, anticipation lighting their eyes at the prospect of having a Christmas tree. A sense of purpose blossomed in her chest. How could she keep such a simple gift from them when she had the chance to do something? "My decorations are sitting unopened in my basement. I'd feel better if someone put them to use. Do you have a place to set up the tree?"

Shawna set her fork down and looked at the quiet pleading in her children's faces. A slow nod set her curls in motion. "We're staying in an apartment right now. It's tight, but we could make room." She glanced at Taryn and chewed her lower lip, her voice cautious. "But only if you're sure."

The elderly man from the store crossed Taryn's mind—the way he'd insisted she accept his gift, the look of merriment in his gaze when he'd asked her to let him be a blessing.

A smile curved her mouth and a weightless feeling lifted her spirits. "I'm sure."

LATER THAT AFTERNOON, TARYN CLIMBED IN HER JEEP Cherokee to deliver the tree. At the end of the Christmas event, she'd gotten Shawna's phone number and address and promised to come by as soon as she could. With the help of a neighbor, she'd loaded the bulky box into the back of her SUV and added other boxes of decorations.

Anticipation pulsed through her as she made the fifteen-minute drive to the apartment complex Shawna and her kids called home. The sun shone bright today, turning the snow into a glittery blanket, and Taryn imagined the children's expressions would be just as bright once they put up the tree.

She parked in front of Shawna's building and found her unit on the first floor. Within seconds of her knock, the door opened and Shawna gave her a cheery greeting. "Come in. Welcome to our humble home."

Shawna's tropical scent welcomed Taryn inside, and the kids hovered in the background, quietly watching as she viewed the living room on the right and a set of stairs on the left.

"That goes up to the bathroom and bedroom," Shawna said. "The kids sleep up there, and I sleep down here on the couch."

Taryn's gaze shifted to the sofa that sat against the wall of the tiny living room. An old TV sat against the opposite wall, but no other furniture graced the space except a beat-up card table in the adjoining dining area.

"It's close quarters, but we make it work." Shawna shrugged and faced the corner of the room near the couch. "I thought the tree could go there."

"Looks perfect."

The next several minutes were spent lugging the boxes into the apartment, and soon the kids gathered around the Christmas tree box, looking eager to pounce.

A wave of contentment washed through Taryn as she studied the glow on their faces.

"Would you like to help us put up the tree?"

Shawna's question lodged in Taryn's throat, expanding into a lump. A blur of images swirled through her mind—bittersweet memories from Christmases past, the hope and excitement on the children's faces in front of her.

No, she needed to give this family the space to make their own memories. Giving Shawna a reassuring smile, she shook her head. "I need to get home and check on my dog. I've neglected him today." As she turned for the door, she reached inside her coat pocket, seeking her keys. But her fingers met a thick piece of paper instead. The kindness card.

She'd meant to give it to Shawna at church this morning, but they'd gotten caught up in the busyness of the event. Now, as her hand brushed the card, she knew it was time.

With quaking fingers, she extracted it from her pocket and handed it to Shawna. She held her breath as Shawna read the words, her face registering surprise, then understanding, and finally a glimmer of hope.

Shawna's eyes filled with tears, and she wrapped Taryn in a hug, her voice thick. "How can I ever thank you?"

Taryn drew back and offered a shaky smile. "Just do what the card says and pass it on."

Shawna sniffed and nodded. "I will."

The kids asked their mom for help opening one of the boxes, and Taryn took it as her cue to say good-bye and slip out.

The drive home passed quickly as her mind stayed on Shawna and the kids, making brief jaunts to Michael and their far-too-short marriage. Shawna had found contentment outside her possessions. Could

Taryn find peace even if she never saw her wedding ring again? Michael had been right—the ring didn't define their relationship. What defined it was the memories they'd shared, the commitment they'd made to love each other in sickness and in health.

She pulled onto her street and took in the Christmas lights that lined her neighbors' homes. She wasn't quite ready yet to deck out her house, but her melancholy was finally starting to lift.

She parked the Jeep and entered the house, grinning when Samson bounded toward her with his usual greeting. She bent down and ruffled the fur between his ears. "Did you have fun today?" He wriggled closer and licked her hand.

"Probably not as much fun as I had." She gave him a final pat and stood, her heart lightening as she took off her coat and stepped into the kitchen.

The click of Samson's nails trailed on the linoleum behind her, and she topped off his food and water. While he set to work filling his stomach, Taryn settled at the table with her phone and looked up the church staff directory in search of Joyce's number. She had to tell the sweet woman what God had done today.

Once she'd found Joyce's information and placed the call, it rang four times before switching to voice mail. Taryn set down her phone with a sigh. Now what to do?

Joyce's verse from the Christmas party teased Taryn's memory, but before she could search for her Bible, her phone buzzed against the table. Was Joyce returning her call already? Instead, an unfamiliar number appeared at the top of a text message.

It's Shawna. Can you come over? It's important.

Taryn's brows bunched together as she tried to decipher the message. What was so important that she needed to go straight there? *Everything okay?*

Yes. Have a surprise you need to see. Come whenever you can.

Taryn's curiosity spiked, but Shawna didn't seem in a hurry to uncover the mystery over the phone. Samson jumped into Taryn's lap and snuggled against her as she tapped in her reply. *Be there in twenty minutes.*

She set her phone on the table and stroked Samson's back, her mind drumming up possibilities of what Shawna had in store. Most likely, she wanted Taryn to see the decorated tree, and this was a sneaky way to include her in their family festivities.

Taryn would find out soon enough. She picked up Samson and carried him to the couch, smiling when he gave a dejected whine, then nestled into the cushion for a nap. After shrugging into her coat and grabbing her purse, she headed back to the apartment complex.

This time when Shawna opened the door, a secretive glint sparkled in her eyes. "Come on in."

Taryn ignored the ratchet in her pulse and stepped inside to see the Christmas tree standing in the corner, the children beaming as they put the finishing touches on it. Lights twinkled from every branch, and a rush of memories flooded her as she noted each of the ornaments she'd received as gifts or bought. At the top of the tree, her frilly white angel stood guard, smiling down on the gathering. Taryn pressed her lips together and struggled to find her voice. "It's beautiful."

"Really transforms the place, doesn't it?" Without waiting for an answer, Shawna walked to the kitchen, talking over her shoulder as she went. "That's not why I had you come over, though."

A partial wall hid Shawna once she'd entered the kitchen, and Taryn wiped her palms on her jeans. What was going on?

When Shawna emerged, she hid her hands behind her back, and a playful grin lifted her mouth. "We found something in the bottom of the Christmas tree box, and I have a hunch it might mean a lot to you. I was pulling out a big branch, and next thing I knew, something pinged against the TV..."

Shawna swung her hand in front of her and uncurled her fingers. Taryn's heart stopped.

Her wedding ring.

Emotion surged to her eyes as she took it from Shawna and ran her thumb and index finger over every curve, feeling the edges of the diamond and marveling at the way the tree lights made it sparkle and dance.

It was in the Christmas tree box. Can you believe it, Michael? After all the times they'd searched that box, thinking the ring might've fallen off when they'd taken down the tree. But it'd never shown up. It must have been buried in one of the branches.

Tears blurred her vision as she slid the ring on her finger, the feel of it reconnecting her to the man she'd loved and lost.

How long would it have stayed hidden if a young woman hadn't delivered cookies to an elderly man? If he hadn't offered his generosity to a stranger at the grocery store? She wouldn't have received the kindness card that encouraged her to step out of her comfort zone to host a family in need and offer them her Christmas tree. And she would have missed this divine moment.

"Though you have made me see troubles, many and bitter, you will restore my life again; from the depths of the earth you will again bring me up." The verse rang again in Taryn's mind as her smile broke free. All this time she'd thought isolation would help her heal from the pain of her husband's death, would shield her from further scars. But maybe the key to restoring her life wasn't found in introspection alone, but in letting God use her to meet the needs of others.

A ring of kindness that had come full circle.

CHRISTMAS DREAMS

Ashley Clark

*L*oretta Rae hadn't planned to be in the kitchen, baking pies at dawn on Christmas morning—and yet that's precisely where she found herself. Wearing a gingerbread-man apron, she watched through the window as a vibrant cardinal carried Christmas tidings to the backyards of Fairhope, Alabama. There was something sweet and fresh about the stillness of the morning that would soon be lost in the hustle and bustle of the rest of the day.

Loretta hummed "It's Beginning to Look a Lot like Christmas" as she whisked pecans into the sugary mixture. Her son Alex would be happy she was making his favorite chocolate pecan pie. And this year, her youngest grandchild would even be old enough to try a piece. It seemed only yesterday that Alex was the youngest child at Christmas gatherings. How her family had grown since then.

Continuing to whisk, Loretta looked to the framed photograph of her husband that hung next to her china cabinet and sighed. "Oh, Henry. If only you were around to see this." Today would have marked their fifty-fifth anniversary. Ten years had passed since Henry's passing, but her heart still longed for him so much that it might as well have been yesterday. Loretta wiped the tears from her eyes with a kitchen towel and used a gingham oven mitt to slide the pecan pie onto the top rack of the preheated oven.

There. That would do just fine. The pie was in the oven; the ham should be nearly thawed in the refrigerator. She set the timer for an hour and went to work whipping potatoes and shredding cheese for the macaroni.

Her white-and-black cocker spaniel caught the scent of the food and made her way into the kitchen. She yawned and stretched on her front two paws before settling down again to watch Loretta.

The oven timer sounded. Loretta slipped the oven mitt back onto her hand and pulled the pie from the rack. It was crisped to perfection. She could hardly wait to see the look on her son's face when she handed him a slice.

Speaking of which, their plane should be leaving any time now from Colorado. Alex, his wife, Chelsea, and their son, Graham, had taken a trip this year to spend the week before Christmas with Chelsea's family in Colorado. They had read Christmas stories by the fireside and gone sledding down a snowy white hill.

Oh, how Loretta envied their white Christmas! The only snow she'd ever seen had been on television, magazines, and those photographs her northern friends kept sharing on Facebook. What she would do for just five minutes of snowfall. Five minutes—that was all she was asking.

The few times it had snowed in southern Alabama during her lifetime, she'd been away. Wouldn't you know that would be her luck? She was just sure her son and daughter-in-law were having a wonderful time with Chelsea's family.

But let's face it—Denver was no Alabama. And nobody cooked Christmas dinner like Loretta Rae. So Alex had insisted they'd arrive in time for Christmas dinner, and said he'd do his best to bring along a little snow.

But chilly as this Christmas morning might be, sunlight warmed the low branches of the old oak tree outside Loretta's kitchen window. Loretta's chances of seeing snow on her seventy-sixth Christmas were about as rotten as they'd always been. Why, she was more likely to see a hurricane on Christmas than snow.

Loretta measured flour for her sugar cookies and poured it into the same large green Tupperware bowl she'd been using for the past forty years. The phone rang, and the bag escaped from her grasp. At least two extra heaps of flour poofed onto the counter.

Phooey. So much for trying to keep the kitchen clean while she worked.

Loretta grabbed the corded phone, the taste of flour on her lips. "Hello?"

"Hey, Mom. Merry Christmas."

"Alex! Merry Christmas to you." Loretta wiped her hands on her apron and turned with the phone to lean against the kitchen counter. She glanced at the clock on the stove. "Wait—aren't you about to board your plane?"

A long pause prefaced his answer. "Well, that's the thing. I'm afraid I've got some bad news."

Loretta bit her lip and looked at the feast she'd already prepared, spread out across the kitchen countertops. "Go on."

"You remember I told you about all the snowfall here yesterday?"

"*Mm-hmm.*" She remembered all right. She'd spent the rest of the evening trying to curb her jealousy.

"Apparently, Colorado's in the middle of a snowstorm. And we get to watch it from the airport terminal." He sighed, his frustration clear. "Our flight was delayed. I wish there was something I could do, Mom." He was silent for a moment. "I'm so sorry. I know how much Christmas dinner means to you."

"Don't worry, Alex. Really. You just focus on enjoying Christmas morning with your family as best you can. Stay safe, okay?" Loretta closed her eyes, hoping her tone masked her disappointment.

"Mom, you haven't already cooked, have you?"

Loretta raised an eyebrow and clutched the phone a little tighter. "Are you kidding? At seven o'clock in the morning?"

"Oh, good. I'd hate for you to have gone to all that work for nothing."

Loretta gulped. "Tell me about it."

"Well, I'd better get back to Chelsea and Graham. Thanks for understanding. Again, merry Christmas, Mom. I love you."

"I love you too, Chipmunk."

Loretta waited for the dial tone and hung up the phone. She looked around at the flour-scattered room. The closest she would get to a white Christmas.

She could've slid down to the floor in a puddle of tears. But if she gave in to that temptation, she faced two problems. One, it would take quite a lot of effort to get back up. And two, she'd be going directly against her own mama's advice: "Save your tears for happy occasions—you only get so much heart to give."

Didn't matter that Loretta Rae was seventy-six years old. A daughter always listens to her mother. And Loretta's mother was liable to strike her from the grave if she didn't.

Truth be told, that was also the only reason that kept Loretta from vacuuming in those little crevices behind the kitchen table. She was pretty sure Jesus didn't care if there were a few crumbs over there.

So Loretta wet a few paper towels to wipe the flour from the counters and set to work cleaning things up. Having a pity party wouldn't change anything. Like it or not, it seemed she would be spending Christmas alone, with a feast large enough to feed a small village.

What she *really* needed right now was a few Christmas carols to keep her company. Loretta moved to her formal room toward the still-working record player, then put on an old Louis Armstrong Christmas record. The needle skipped once before settling into the worn grooves as Loretta swayed back and forth to the familiar tune.

As the song reached its chorus, memories flooded back. Memories of the many Christmases Loretta and her younger sister had danced to this very song—their father's favorite.

How many years since they'd spoken to one another? Could it really be...forty?

Loretta had never meant to be the kind of person who cuts off a family member. Truly, she hadn't. But she'd been so fiercely angry at Violet when—fifteen years into her marriage—she'd found out what her sister had done. She just didn't know how she could forgive her. On the eve of Loretta's wedding day, no less. And on Christmas Eve.

Loretta probably never would've found out either, had she not discovered Violet's letters in their mother's house. Loretta's husband, Henry—always the protector—had shielded her from it, thinking he was saving her grief. Oh, she'd been mad as a bat at him too, at first. Not in public, of course. But in private, Loretta burned his grilled cheese sandwiches for weeks.

But over time, she came to realize she had no reason to blame her husband. Henry had done nothing wrong—nothing, except for keeping Violet's secret. But he did it for the sake of their family, and Loretta loved him for that.

Her sister, on the other hand, was a different story. Really—coming to Henry's apartment on the eve of Loretta's wedding day and professing her love for him like a woman with loose morals?

Loretta shook her head and made her way back into the kitchen. It was a shame she'd lost touch with her sister. But after all these years, she didn't know how she could even begin to make up for the lost time. Not to mention Violet still owed her one big, fat apology.

She sighed. There were still so many things she wanted to do in her life. Making peace with Violet was only one of them. She'd always wanted to dance in a park, for instance. And she never had made it to Italy, or tried those chestnuts she'd heard about for years in the Christmas carol.

"God," she whispered, "am I too old for all that? Is it time for me to let go of far-fetched dreams?"

When He didn't answer immediately, Loretta figured it best to lower her expectations. This Christmas had already turned out so very different from what she'd thought it would be.

Loretta scooped the macaroni and cheese and mashed potatoes into containers, and checked the pie to see if it was yet cool enough to put in the fridge. As she transferred all the food onto the refrigerator shelves, the half-made sugar cookies caught her eye.

Well, she may as well salvage them. No sense in letting good cookies go to waste. She rummaged through the refrigerator for the egg carton but found only the one she'd just emptied. Didn't that beat all?

Loretta closed the door to the fridge, careful not to knock the magnets holding her grandson's school picture. She'd have to phone her neighbor.

"Hello, Susan? This is Loretta." Loretta scratched remnants of flour from her fingernails.

"Merry Christmas!" Their house sounded hectic in the background.

"Merry Christmas to you too! Say, I was wondering. Do you have a couple eggs I could borrow?"

Loretta heard a refrigerator open on Susan's side of the line. "*Hmm...*I'm looking through the shelves right here, and you know, I must have used the last one in my corn casserole just now."

So much for sugar cookies. "That's okay. Thanks for check—"

"Loretta, wait. My nephew is in town from college, and I can tell he's just dying to get a few minutes away from the mayhem around here. Why don't I send him over, and he can take you up to the store?"

"Nonsense. I don't want to disrupt your family time."

Susan laughed. "Believe me, you'd be doing him a favor."

"Well, if you insist." Loretta smiled. Somehow, redeeming the sugar cookies made her feel like a little part of this Christmas could be salvaged after all. "Thanks, Susan."

"You bet."

Loretta hung up the phone and set to work cleaning up the rest of the flour from the floor. Then she took a quick glance in the mirror as she untied her apron.

"Yikes," she murmured. How had she managed to streak so much flour through her dyed-auburn hair? She hurried off to the bathroom and ran a hairbrush through her stylish bob. With a pinch of blush to her cheeks and a little red lipstick, she was good as new. And just in the nick of time too. As soon as she finished tidying up, the doorbell rang.

She opened the front door wide to see a dashing young man who appeared to be in his early twenties. His dark hair was cropped in a Cary Grant style, and he wore a cashmere sweater and jeans. If only Loretta had a granddaughter...

"Hello." He shook her hand, a winsome smile on his face. "I'm William."

"Loretta Rae."

"Pleasure to make your acquaintance." William turned his head and pointed toward the formal sitting area. "Is that Louis Armstrong I hear?"

Loretta patted him on the back, then closed the door. Yes, they were going to get along just fine this afternoon. "Sure is—I've had that record for twice as long as you've been alive."

"Maybe I'm older than I look." William's eyes twinkled as he made his way toward the record player. He whistled and ran his finger along the edge. "Mint condition."

"Well, as mint as something can be when it's old as dirt." Loretta walked into the kitchen to retrieve her purse from the counter, then joined him back in the sitting area. "I truly appreciate your taking the time to run a crazy old woman up to the store."

"For starters," William said, "you're not old. I can already tell you're sprightly as a squirrel, from the glint in your eye. And secondly, it'll be a pleasure to escort you on this lovely Christmas morning."

Loretta slung her late mother's Grace Kelly–style purse over her arm and led William toward the door. Her dog's paws clattered from the kitchen.

"We'll be back in a little while, Sugar," Loretta said. The spaniel took a seat beside the door, her large eyes drooping with reproach.

"Don't mind her." Loretta opened the door for William. "I swear, that dog has me trained rather than the other way around. If I had a penny for every time she made me give her a treat…"

William laughed and took Loretta's keys to secure the door behind them. He unlocked the car and opened the passenger side door for Loretta. She hugged her sweater a little closer to her body, chilled from the cool winter temperature.

"Well, aren't you a gentleman." Loretta slid inside and set her purse down on the freshly vacuumed floor mat.

William climbed in, shut his door, and rapped his fingertips along the steering wheel. He turned to Loretta. "I've heard there's a grocery store about fifteen minutes away that's open. Sound good?"

"Indeed." Her gaze traveled to the red garland draped along the white porch of her historic Fairhope home and the containers of poinsettias lining the walkway. Alex's boy, Graham, had helped her plant those flowers in preparation for Christmas. She sighed. Such a shame they couldn't be here today.

William pulled out from her curved driveway and onto the neighborhood street, as sunlight filtered through the sweeping oak limbs. Children in a nearby yard stopped on their bicycles to wave from their driveway.

Oh, to be young again, and still full of dreams.

"Hey, I heard there's a Christmas festival going on in the park. Do we have time to stop by?" William pulled up to the stop sign and turned his attention to Loretta, his eyebrows raised.

Loretta fiddled with the bracelet Alex and Chelsea had given her last Christmas. "We have time, but I couldn't ask you to do that." Her gaze traveled to the window, where she caught a glimpse of a little girl wearing a brand-new princess costume, twirling around in her yard.

"I assure you, Loretta, it's no bother at all. I'd love to see the festival myself."

A few moments later, William pulled into the grassy park where rows of booths proved they'd found the festival. Teenage girls wearing huge pastel antebellum-themed dresses waved as they walked by the car on their way toward the festival.

William blinked a few times. "Were those girls wearing what I think they were wearing?"

Loretta chuckled. "I take it you haven't spent much time in the South."

"Clearly not enough." William switched off the ignition and helped Loretta out of his car.

"Those girls are called the Azalea Trail Maids. Their group goes back nearly one hundred years and gets its name from an azalea trail in Mobile, up the road from here." Loretta fiddled with her pearl earrings as they walked toward the festival.

The smell of toasted cinnamon almonds made Loretta's stomach grumble as they approached. Somehow, in the mayhem of that cooking this morning, she'd completely forgotten breakfast.

William must have followed her gaze to the tent selling the almonds. "Would you like some?" He pulled out his wallet, ready to spring into action.

Loretta waved away his money. "You were kind enough to drive me to this festival. The least I can do is buy us a snack."

"Well, all right." William smiled. "If you insist."

Next in line, Loretta approached the cash register, her attention still on the list of offered items. Wait a second. Boiled chestnuts on the menu? Okay, so they weren't the roasted ones from the song, but... *God, are you trying to tell me something? That's one of my bucket list dreams.*

"Ma'am," the man behind the counter prompted, "do you know what you'd like?"

"Yes." Loretta loosened the metal clasp of her purse. "I'll have one order of roasted almonds and one order of boiled chestnuts, please." She handed him the exact amount in cash for both.

The man scooped their snacks into paper cones and handed them to Loretta and William with a smile. "There you are."

Loretta reached to take her chestnuts, careful none of them spilled over the paper.

"Have a merry Christmas!" the young man called out.

William waved back at him as they turned to leave. "You too." He tossed an almond into his mouth. "Mmm. Delicious."

Loretta looked down at her chestnuts, then took a sniff of them. Live music drew her attention away from the chestnuts and toward the band seated around the park fountain. Loretta found herself humming along with "Silver Bells."

"How are your chestnuts?" William asked.

"Well, truth be told . . ." Loretta picked one up from the paper cone to examine it. The chestnut was somehow more . . . boiled . . . than she'd imagined. "I haven't exactly tried any yet."

"Have you had them before?"

Loretta shook her head and dared a bite.

"Well, how is it?"

Loretta swallowed and crinkled her nose. Yikes.

"That bad?" William laughed.

"Tastes like a mushy chestnut."

William held the almonds out to her. "Here. Why don't you take these?"

"No," Loretta said, the familiar smell of the cinnamon almonds tempting her despite her words. "I couldn't do that."

William continued to grin as he held out the almonds to her.

"Well, if you want the boiled chestnuts so badly, I won't make you beg me." Shamelessly, Loretta switched with him and ate a handful of the almonds.

William laughed and tossed the chestnuts into a garbage can. "Let me know if you want to browse inside any of these booths."

"Actually—" Loretta stopped and ate another handful of the almonds. "These pashminas are lovely. Would you mind if I took a glance?"

"Not at all." William eyed the paper cup in her hand. "I don't suppose I could have a few more of those almonds...?"

Loretta grinned and handed him the rest. "You take them. I'm done."

She stepped into the booth while William meandered around outside in the sunshine. The varying colors of pashminas were stunning. Loretta checked for a price sticker but instead found a tag that read, *Imported from Italy*.

First the boiled chestnuts, and now her own little trip to Italy?

Loretta chose one of the scarves with a striking ocean color, then waved for the sales attendant's attention. "Excuse me, ma'am," she said. "How much for this one?"

The woman had an air of familiarity about her. Loretta couldn't quite place it... until she turned.

Loretta had to catch her breath. "Violet?"

Her sister stood frozen, her eyes wide in surprise. "Loretta?"

Loretta hadn't seen her in at least ten years. The last time she'd spotted her sister, Violet was eating at Panini Pete's, and Loretta had slipped into an art gallery before Violet could see her. Loretta hadn't felt strong that day. Certainly not strong enough to face her sister.

For years, Loretta had imagined what she might say to Violet if she saw her again. She'd looked in the mirror and pretended to explain to Violet the depth of her frustration, anger, and disappointment at Violet's betrayal. She'd cried and raged. And yet, in this moment, all Loretta could think was how badly she wanted to hug her dear sister.

But Violet got to her before Loretta could. "Oh, Loretta," Violet said, her words choked with tears. "I'm so very sorry." She pulled back from the hug to look Loretta straight in the eyes. "I must've picked up the phone a thousand times to call you, but nothing I could say ever seemed adequate. I never should've gone to Henry that night before your wedding. I was so immature and naive. Could you ever find it in your heart to forgive me?"

Loretta's hands trembled as she reached to hold onto her sister's arms. "Dear, dear Violet, I never should've let this go on so long. The Bible tells us to forgive seventy times seven, yet I've made excuse after excuse to stay angry with you. Perhaps you are the one who ought to forgive me."

A rush of happy tears flowed from Loretta's eyes. She was free from a weight she hadn't realized she'd been carrying, and she felt a truer joy than she had in years.

Violet folded up the pashmina and handed it to Loretta. "Here. Consider this my Christmas present to you."

Loretta ran her finger around the delicate edge. "Thank you, Violet."

Several people walked into the booth, picking up various scarves and trying them on. Loretta hugged the pashmina to her heart and squeezed Violet's hand. "I'll let you get back to work. Call me when you get off, okay? We have a lot to catch up on."

Violet smiled. "Yes, indeed." She squeezed Loretta's hand right back. "I hope you know I love you."

Loretta closed her eyes, peace sweeping over her as she returned her sister's smile with her own wide grin. "Merry Christmas, Violet. I love you too."

As she stepped out of the booth and looked for William, Loretta wrapped her new pashmina around her neck and tied it snugly. She wiped a few stray tears from her eyes and checked for mascara streaks.

When she spotted William, he was standing near the live band and waved her over. "Loretta, over here!"

The band began to play "Rockin' around the Christmas Tree," and Loretta found herself tapping her foot along with the beat.

William pointed toward the band. "They're pretty good, huh? While you were shopping, they said they're actually high schoolers."

"Pretty impressive." Loretta couldn't help the smile on her face. Had she really just reunited with her sister after all these years?

William took notice of Loretta's tapping foot. "Would you like to dance?"

Loretta looked back at the band and gulped. She hadn't really thought about it before now, but this *was* a park, and she *had* always wanted to dance in one. But dancing with a man young enough to be her grandson? What would people think? She looked down at her vibrant new Italian pashmina, and it gave her courage. "You know," she said, lifting her chin, "I would like that very much."

Loretta slid her purse up to her shoulder to keep it from smacking William, and took his outstretched hand. He helped her balance with his other hand behind her shoulder. Slowly, he showed her how to rock step to the beat.

She looked him straight in the eyes, her new scarf working wonders to keep her warm. "Have you studied ballroom dancing?"

William gave her a mysterious look. "Have you?"

Loretta nearly snorted. "Why? Because I'm graceful as a swan?"

William spun her, and Loretta stretched out her arm with flair. "You sure seem to know what you're doing."

"Let's just say I watch *a lot* of dancing shows on television." She winked at him. "But that's our secret. We'll let everyone else think I may actually have experience dancing."

"Well, you could've fooled me."

She swatted his arm. "Oh, you are a charmer, I'll give you that. And a mighty good dancer too, I might add."

"So tell me," William asked, "have you ever danced in a park to a Christmas carol before?"

Loretta laughed. "Can't say I have." She leaned a little closer and whispered, "Truth be told, I haven't danced since my thirties. Well, really *danced*, that is. I suppose I twirl around my kitchen by myself all the time."

"I'd say that counts as dancing." He spun her again for a big finish as the band ended the song.

"William?" Loretta squeezed his hand and took one last glance at the band.

"Yes, Loretta?"

"If I tell you something, do you promise not to think I'm crazy?"

"I can't make any promises..." He winked in jest.

Loretta rolled her eyes. "I'm serious!" She ran her fingers along the pashmina at her neck. "It's just...all these things have been happening to me today."

William frowned. "What kind of things?"

Loretta held up her hands to explain. "Oh, good things. I should've said that. Definitely good things. See, this is where the crazy part comes in. You'll never believe this, but before you showed up at my house, I was feeling pretty down about my son's flight being delayed. And, well—I guess I started to think that maybe I was too old for all those silly dreams I've carried in my heart since I was a girl. You know, dreams like dancing in a park or trying boiled chestnuts. Little things, I guess, but they're the things that give life color. So I asked God if I was getting too old for all those fancies—if maybe it was time to give up my dreams. And then—would you believe it?—you showed up, and here we are, at this Christmas festival."

William studied her with a deep sort of kindness in his eyes. "Loretta Rae?"

"Yes?"

"I don't think that's crazy at all."

In that moment, Loretta could've cried. It was probably silly. To any other person, this afternoon would've just been a fun few hours at a Christmas festival. But for Loretta, it meant so much more.

Loretta waved to Violet as they walked past her booth, then took hold of William's elbow while Violet was still watching. No harm in hamming it up a bit, was there? A woman had to take advantage of these situations as they came to her.

As they walked through the festival, a thought occurred to Loretta. In one fell swoop, William just helped her fulfill all her bucket-list dreams!

Maybe she should've given God a little more to work with. That settled it. When she got home, she was sitting down with her Bible and a pad of paper to work on a whole new list of dreams.

"We'd better get you those eggs you need so you have time to finish your cookies," William said. He looked up to the gentle sky as small clouds began to form above them.

"Sounds good to me." Loretta opened the door to her side of the car, and William helped her in.

An hour later, Loretta and William had purchased the eggs as well as a few other last-minute groceries and made it back to Loretta's front porch. Loretta took a seat on her hanging porch swing as the clouds began to roll in.

"I sure do appreciate you taking me to the store—and to the festival," she said. She gently rocked back and forth on the well-worn wooden swing. "It means more to me than you know."

William nodded. "Don't mention it."

"Guess you'd better get back," Loretta said.

William looked up towards the ever-greying sky and smiled. "Yeah, guess I'd better."

He walked over to Loretta and pulled her up from the swing, into a hug. She still missed her own grandson, but this guy was a welcome substitute.

Loretta picked her grocery bag up from the ground and unlocked the front door of her cottage home. She watched William as he took the couple steps down her porch.

"William?"

He turned to face her. "Yes, Loretta?"

"I sure hope we get a chance to chat again someday."

A half-grin slid up his face. "Something tells me we will."

Loretta closed the door behind her and smiled, warmed from the inside out. She headed straight toward the kitchen to refrigerate the eggs, and preheated the oven for the ham.

What an unexpectedly wonderful Christmas this had become. And to think—it had started with such disappointment!

She should call Susan immediately to thank her for sharing William. Loretta put her baking apron back on, then dialed Susan's number. "Susan? This is Loretta."

"Oh, Loretta!" Susan sounded frazzled, and Loretta could just picture her with all those children running around. "I hope you can hear me over the awful racket everyone is making. See, I wanted to make a special Christmas dinner this year, but I'm afraid in all the mayhem, I ruined the turkey. Now I'm horrified. It seems I've ruined Christmas for everyone."

"You know," Loretta said, "I happen to have more than enough food over here. Including a Christmas ham. I'd be thrilled to share it with you."

Susan breathed a huge sigh. "You're a lifesaver, you know that?"

Loretta smiled. Seemed she wouldn't be eating a Christmas feast by herself after all. Amazing how God worked out all the little details—especially when she let go of trying to make things perfect.

"I mean it, Loretta. You are a gift to us. And I feel just awful. Things got so hectic around here, it completely slipped my mind to send my nephew over there."

"Wait a second." Loretta stilled. "What do you mean, you forgot to send your nephew?"

The kitchen timer went off on Susan's side of the line, and Loretta could've sworn she heard the smoke detector beep. "You asked for eggs earlier, and I promised to send him over. In all the chaos, I completely forgot."

"But…" Loretta thought of William's sparkling smile when he showed up at her porch, and his final glance at the cloudy sky before departing. "I don't understand. What about William?"

"Who's William?" Susan asked.

Loretta was beginning to wonder that herself.

A chirping sparrow drew her attention to the large kitchen window, and suddenly, Loretta nearly dropped the telephone. She couldn't believe her eyes. "Susan, I'm going to need to call you back." Loretta hung up the phone and rushed out the back door of her cottage home.

Her face toward the sky, Loretta spread her arms wide. It was snowing. In Fairhope, Alabama.

She tugged her pashmina a little closer, and noticed for the first time that it was embroidered. She squinted to make out the words: *For he will command his angels concerning you to guard you in all your ways.—Psalm 91:11*

Suddenly, it all made sense. The visit from William. The boiled chestnuts. The dance in the park. Violet…

As she looked up into the sky, snowflakes fell to her cheeks and nose, blanketing the ground in a fluffy covering of white. And Loretta Rae smiled. Because she knew in that moment that the dreams of a seventy-six-year-old widow matter very much to God. Just as each unique snowflake mattered as it cascaded to the ground.

HERE WE COME
A-WASSAILING

Anita Mae Draper

*J*oan Rigler took a final walk around her cozy
bungalow. Furnace turned low? Check. Lines
to the water main closed? Check. Appliances
off and cell phone charger packed? Check. Check.

Weather reports of slick roads and numerous acci-
dents in the Minot, North Dakota, area had given her a
tough choice: drive for hours in snowy, icy conditions
or leave her widowed mom to spend Christmas alone.
Since the latter thought had made her heart lurch, she
had remote-started her new SUV—a gift she'd bought
herself on her thirtieth birthday with money her
father had left in his will—and let the engine warm up
in preparation for her road trip.

The second that Joan stepped outside, her cell phone vibrated before breaking out into a muffled chorus of "Here We Come A-Wassailing," her Christmas ringtone. She hurried her house keys from the dead bolt and exchanged them for her phone.

"On my way, Mom," she said, walking with caution to her SUV.

"Are you sure, Joanie? The weatherman said it's bad out there."

"Yes, but it'll take longer than normal. Promise you'll give me at least five hours before you start worrying. And I'll probably lose coverage if they haven't got those new cell phone towers online yet."

"Okay, honey. Drive safe, now. I'll be praying for you."

"Thanks, Mom. I'll see you soon. Love you." Saying good-bye to Mom was getting harder every time. But did she have to say good-bye? Maybe it was time to move back home. With the current efficiency of couriers, her transcribing service could be done from any location. And if Mom was as lonely as she was at times, living together would benefit them both.

Darkness descended as she drove toward the bypass on South Broadway, surprised to see so many people still out on the roads.

She cranked up the Christmas music playing over the SUV's speakers, only to hear an unfamiliar alert signal shrill through them. Adrenaline shot through her system, throwing her into a momentary panic, until a glance at her dashboard display reminded her it was an incoming call. Heart thumping, she pressed the answer button on her steering wheel. "On my way, Mom," she called out to ensure the hidden microphone picked up her voice.

"It's Miranda. Where are you? Are you on the road yet?"

Joan merged onto the western bypass. "Almost. Why?"

"My car won't start," her best friend's voice wailed through the speakers. "And I should have been at my sister's hours ago."

Joan wasn't surprised. Only two years younger than Joan, Miranda had a penchant for getting into scrapes. Missing her family's Christmas reunion would be a heart-wrencher, though. A few more minutes wouldn't hurt. "Hang tight and I'll swing by for you."

As it turned out, picking Miranda up wasn't the problem—it was dropping her off in the empty driveway of a dark house on Christmas Eve. "Maybe they're hiding inside, ready to yell, 'Surprise!'" Joan ventured.

Miranda didn't answer. She scoured through her oversize handbag and withdrew a cherry-red phone. After several moments of searching her e-mail, she stopped abruptly and stared at the screen. "They l-left without me..." Her eyes pooled.

Joan handed her a tissue. "Aww, sweetie, they couldn't have."

"Yes, they would have. I'm late for everything and here, look—" She held up her cell phone so Joan could read the e-mail. "My sister said to be here by four o'clock if I wanted a ride with them."

The dashboard clock glowed 5:05.

"So, what do you want to do?"

Miranda dabbed under her mascara-lined eyes with shaking fingers. "I don't know. Call a taxi and go back h-home, I guess."

Time was passing and Joan had a very long way to go. "The taxi would cost too much. Why don't you spend Christmas with me and Mom?"

Miranda looked skeptical. "She wouldn't mind? Christmas is for families."

"Families *and* friends." Joan backed out of the driveway. "And no, she wouldn't mind at all." Yet even as she said the words, an uncomfortable childhood memory surfaced. She shook her head at the thought and pushed it down. Her mother shouldn't be remembered for one unsocial act a long time ago.

A TOWERING SIGN ON THE FREEWAY SHONE THROUGH the flurries like a homing beacon. After checking for oncoming vehicles, Joan steered into the entrance of a truck stop. They were lucky to find someplace open on Christmas Eve.

A few minutes later she sat at one of two small tables, drinking coffee with Miranda. "I don't know how truckers do it at times like this," Joan said.

The snort of a loud truck braking on the service road drew her attention through the reflected image on the window. Within seconds, the truck revved up and pulled away without parking. A young girl with long hair streaming sideways in the wind trudged across the road, wearing a vintage baseball jacket instead of a winter coat. She entered the truck stop and disappeared from view.

"How long before we get to Fiska?" Miranda asked.

"We're about a quarter of the way there. Slow driving in this weather."

Miranda shivered. "I counted three vehicles in the ditch already."

"At least the sheriff's department is on top of it. Tow trucks will be busy tonight."

"Well, I have faith in your driving and God's hand upon the wheel." Miranda smiled, then stood. "Be right back."

As Miranda excused herself, the girl in the baseball jacket plopped into a seat at the empty table next to

Joan. She stared at Joan's foam cup as if she could absorb every ounce through telepathy.

Joan held up her cup. "Would you like a hot chocolate? I'll buy. No strings attached."

Startled wide eyes glanced at Joan and then looked away. She shook her head.

As if on cue, the pudgy employee who had ignored them until now left his post at the till and walked toward them. He wasn't a big man, but with his crossed arms, wide stance, and lowered chin, he had the bearing of a tough New York cop. "Ya gonna buy somethin'? This ain't no hangout."

The girl cowered in her chair.

"All right, out ya go." He made a grab for her arm.

"Don't you dare!" Pulse racing, Joan rose to her full five feet six inches, putting her eye to eye with the man. "You can't put her outside in this kind of weather. She'll freeze."

He looked Joan over slowly. "It's Christmas Eve. I'm closin' soon, and I got my rights." His thumb pointed to the yellowed No Loitering sign.

With a muffled cry, the girl rose and stumbled out the door.

Joan's fingernails dug into her closed fists while the employee sauntered back to his till.

Miranda appeared around the end of the chip aisle. She took one look at Joan and asked, "What did I miss?"

"I'll tell you later. Just get a couple more coffees, a hot chocolate, and three subs, and meet me at the car." Joan rushed outside, praying for wisdom and protection. Picking up a hitchhiker was dangerous on both sides. She needed God to allay the fears and instill the trust the situation required.

She found the girl huddled around the corner out of the wind. "My name is Joan Rigler. My friend and I are heading to Fiska. Is there somewhere we can drop you off?"

No response.

Joan shivered from the cold biting her exposed skin. She held the top of her jacket closed with one hand while starting the SUV with the other. "It'll get colder. Do you have somewhere to go?"

A shrug met her words. Then, tentatively, "Are you going near Crosby?"

"Yes, I drive right past it." Joan pressed her lips together to stop the questions crowding the tip of her tongue. "I could drop you off there, if you'd like."

She gave Joan a sidelong glance. "Okay."

"Perfect," Joan responded. She led the girl toward the SUV. It would be easy enough to drop the girl off with family in Crosby and then bring Miranda home to meet Mom.

As Joan adjusted the rear heating controls, the memory of another uninvited guest materialized. She had been ten years old then; her mind had probably exaggerated the incident. She had nothing to worry about. Really.

TWISTING IN HER SEAT, MIRANDA PASSED A SUB AND hot chocolate to the girl behind her. "I'm Miranda."

"Just call me Foster. Everyone else does."

At the sound of plastic being peeled off the sub, Joan glanced in her rearview mirror. Although she didn't have any credentials in the field of social work, she was an ardent supporter and helper of the church youth group. In her limited experience, everything pointed toward Foster being a runaway. But if the girl felt threatened by a barrage of questions, she was likely to take off at the first chance. How could Joan enjoy Christmas knowing Foster was out there in the cold, alone?

As they crossed into Burke County, Joan's glance in the rearview mirror caught Foster looking back. Her eyes had lost their wide, worried look. Was it because someone really was waiting for her in Crosby? If not, what would she do?

With the flurries ceasing, road conditions improved. Transport traffic increased as they neared the corner just south of the border crossing into Canada, and then thinned out as they passed on by. Everything was spaced far apart, including emergency services. So when Joan saw the red lights of a far-ahead vehicle swerve from the right side of the road to the left and back again, she knew she'd have to check it out.

Minutes later, she pulled alongside a man hunched over the back wheel of an ancient pickup. Using her own controls, she partially opened Miranda's window. "Are you all right?"

He rose and turned an attractive face toward them, crinkles around his eyes suggesting someone who spent a majority of time outdoors. "We're fine, but the tire's shot."

At the mention of someone else, Joan scrutinized the pickup's cab and made out the silhouette of a small head. She nodded at the truck. "Have you got a spare? I could shine my lights while you change it."

"Yep, got a spare all right, but it's back in the shop waiting to be patched." He cocked his head and clicked his tongue. "You always think you can put things off till tomorrow."

Joan's heart melted as she caught the melancholy in his voice. She lowered Miranda's window the rest of the way. "We're heading into Crosby. Can we give you two a lift?"

The man nodded and went to his cab.

At the corner of her eye she saw Foster shrink into the corner, her arm along the door as if ready to pop it open. For the first time, Joan was glad of the child lock feature, which kept the rear doors locked unless opened from the front or the outside.

Miranda murmured, "I'll go sit in the back." She got out, and as she rounded the hood of the SUV, a boy of about eight jumped down from the truck cab with a backpack in his arms.

"Come on, this side." Miranda beckoned to the boy. Turning to the man, she added, "You'll be more comfortable in the front."

"I appreciate that." He locked his doors before climbing into the front passenger seat, a small duffle on his lap.

When the man's presence seemed to fill the whole front of the vehicle, the realization suddenly hit Joan that she'd allowed a perfect stranger into her vehicle on a lonely stretch of highway in one of the most remote parts of the state. Panic flaring, she sought Miranda's gaze in the rearview mirror. Miranda smiled serenely back at her from the middle seat. Foster huddled in her corner with her arms crossed.

"I'm Roy," the boy said from behind Joan. "And that's my dad."

Roy's dad glanced at her. "Pardon me. I must've left my manners in my truck. Frank Larson." He held out a large hand toward her.

"What kind of car is this?" Roy asked.

"Hold your horses, son. You ought to ask a pretty lady her name before you talk about the horse she rides."

The warmth on Joan's face didn't come from the car's heater. She couldn't remember the last time a man—handsome or otherwise—referred to her as pretty. She shook his firm hand and introduced herself and the others sharing the ride. After everyone had their seat belts fastened, they were on their way again.

Frank surveyed the dashboard display. "You're packing some heavy hardware with this outfit. How's the mileage?"

"Ugh. Not that great. But I really like the four-wheel drive and all the safety features, especially the backup camera. I'll admit, though, I jump every time the car picks up a call from my cell phone." She sent a quick glance his way. "Speaking of which, did you need to call someone about your truck?"

"I'll take care of it from the motel. I really do appreciate you picking us up like that. Not many people on the road tonight with it being Christmas Eve."

"Isn't there anyone who could come and get you so you wouldn't have to spend Christmas away from home?"

"It's just Roy and me. His mom died awhile back and my folks are gone. I got someone watching the ranch, so there's no need to worry about the stock. We're pretty free to go where we please, Roy and me."

For all his carefree words, Joan could hear the longing that accompanied them.

The white fluorescent letters on the road sign drew Joan like a magnet. Home. Mom and Dad waiting for her on the covered veranda. Except this time Mom would stand alone. She shook off the encroaching sadness. Dad might be gone from this world, but she had no doubts they'd share a sweet reunion in heaven.

Frank turned to her. "Got someone special waiting in Crosby?"

"No, it's just a quick stop and then we're driving on to a little railway town called Fiska, which is about as remote as you can get in the state." She glanced at him. "No matter what the state says, I can't call a place with only a dozen inhabitants a city. It just doesn't fit."

"I guess every state has its quirks." He didn't say anything for several minutes, as if thinking, then added, "So you'll still be on the road close to an hour after Roy and I are tucked into a warm bed?"

She laughed. "Yeah, I guess so, depending on the road."

"Well, that's plain not fair. How am I supposed to relax knowing you're out here in this?"

"Is that one of those cowboy rules?" She knew she was flirting, but couldn't stop herself.

"You bet. It's bad enough you're driving while I'm twiddling my thumbs."

"Twiddle away, cowboy. No one drives my car."

He chuckled, a low rumble vibrating in the air between them.

It'd been years since she'd felt this attuned to a man. Not since she'd had her heart broken. But this man—what did the cowboys say? This man made her want to get back on the horse and try again. She tapped the steering wheel. They'd be in Crosby soon. In his own words, it was plain not fair.

THE LIGHTS OF CROSBY SHONE BRIGHTER THAN JOAN remembered, thanks to the resurging oil boom.

Frank pointed to a new hotel. "Looks like we'll be out of your hair in no time."

"Is that it, Dad? Is that where we're going to spend Christmas?"

In the rearview mirror, Miranda's stark eyes reflected the same compassion Joan felt.

"Sure it is," Frank said with less eagerness than his son had displayed. "We'll rustle up some jerky and jelly beans, watch some Christmas movies on TV, and settle in to wait for Santa Claus."

Roy's boots kicked the back of Joan's seat like a percussionist with a bongo drum. As much as she wanted to tell him to stop before he marked the leather upholstery, she couldn't seem to get the words past the lump in her throat.

"I hope the TV has one of those fire channels," Roy piped up. "We can pretend it's a campfire. Hey! Look at all those trucks."

Joan stopped under the hotel's canopy, having already noticed the parking lot chock-full of dirty white trucks fresh from the oil patch.

Frank latched onto the door handle. "Mind if I leave Roy here until I get things settled?"

"Not at all. We'll count trucks."

He nodded, more serious than she'd seen him all night. "I'll be right back." He walked away, a tall, well-built man with shoulders wide enough to carry the responsibility of one little boy.

Joan turned to Foster. "So where can we drop you off?"

Foster's eyes flared for a second before she reached for the door handle. "Right here is fine. I can walk the rest of the way." She tugged at the latch.

"Nonsense, I've brought you this far. I can certainly drive you the rest of the way."

Foster kept tugging. "Why won't this door open?" She slapped at it as if that would help.

Joan looked to Miranda, who gave a slight shrug.

"Foster," Joan said in a coaxing voice, "is there anyone here for you?"

Foster paused in her tugging. With a groan, she let go of the handle and slumped in the corner. "No."

"And they call you Foster because…," she prompted.

Foster crossed her arms. "Because I'm a foster kid."

"What's a foster kid?" asked Roy with less exuberance than he'd displayed so far.

Foster leaned toward him. "It's a home for kids whose parents died or didn't want them."

"My mom died, but my dad still wants me."

"You're lucky," Foster said. "I don't have a mom or dad. Not real ones, anyway." She plucked at her worn jeans. "They treat me okay, but—I miss my mom…" She stared out the window toward the town.

Joan hooked her arm over the seat. "Why did you mention Crosby?"

"We used to live here before they died."

Joan strained to catch the fading voice as she put the puzzle pieces together. "Are your parents buried here?" she asked softly.

Foster rested her forehead against the window. "Yes."

Miranda looked stricken.

Joan made a quick decision. "Would you like to visit the cemetery tomorrow? I could bring you after Christmas dinner."

"Really?" Foster sat forward, then slumped back again. "Why would you do that for me? I'm a stranger. A runaway."

"Because..." Joan's eyes blurred, and she blinked at the tears. "Because I know what it's like to lose a parent. I would have braved a blizzard to spend one more Christmas with my dad."

"I miss my mom." Roy's wobbly voice reached across the seat back. "She used to sing to me and bake me Christmas cookies that looked like little men."

Behind Joan, Miranda sniffled.

Just then, Frank returned, sliding quickly into the seat, and closing the door against the frigid wind. "They're full up. Let's try the motel."

Joan wondered at the gruffness in his voice but nodded and put the SUV in gear. As they neared the motel, she saw another sea of dingy white trucks, one before every door, and more scattered around the parking lot. On the side of the office, a red neon *No* flashed off and on beside a red *Vacancy*.

"What does that mean, Dad?"

Frank raised his hands from his thighs, then dropped them back down. He swallowed. "It means they're full up, Roy." He turned appealing eyes on Joan. "Would you mind driving around town to see if there's anything else? With this oil boom, there could be another one."

"Sure can." Joan put the SUV in gear again. As they drove the streets of Crosby, she calculated where everyone could sleep if she brought them all home. The thought was ludicrous, of course, because Mom would have a fit, but she couldn't expect Joan to just dump a man, a boy, and a teen on the side of the road and then head home for some holiday merrymaking.

Without Dad, Mom would have toned the festivities down so there wouldn't be the large kettle of mulled cider simmering on the stove, but she always cooked a huge turkey for the leftovers. And it helped that Mom hadn't moved from their big Victorian when Dad died. There'd be plenty of room for everyone. She should phone Mom and let her know. Her thumb paused over the Call button on her steering wheel as she remembered Aunt Belle being turned away all those years ago. What if Mom said no this time? She gripped the steering wheel and replayed the memory of Aunt Belle showing up unannounced on the eve of some event. Mom had caused a scene, calling Aunt Belle inconsiderate before sending her to a hotel.

Frank's voice broke into her thoughts. "You can drop us off here."

They were driving past the empty parking lot of a closed diner. She pulled to the side and looked around. "Where? I don't see anything."

He spread his hands out. "Well, there's nowhere else, is there?"

"Wait!" Miranda called out. "Did you see that? Back up a bit."

Joan backed up until Miranda called out to stop. "There in the back. There's someone digging in the Dumpster."

"So?" Foster asked. "That's nothing."

Foster's bravado reached down into Joan's chest. She wasn't sure which thought disheartened her more—someone digging through a trash bin or a teen thinking it was nothing out of the ordinary.

A woman emerged from the shadows, her long white ponytail trailing over her shoulder. She set a black trash bag on the ground beside her and then bent down, arm outstretched. Out of the darkness behind her a cat high-stepped through the snow, disdain for the white-covered ground showing plainly in the streetlight's glow. It wolfed down the offering in a flash, took a quick sniff at the ground, and then proceeded to rub the side of its cheek against the woman's bare hand. She straightened, and the cat brushed its body against her legs.

Before Joan defined her thought, she was out of the SUV and striding through the bitter wind toward the woman. A car door *thunked* behind her. A moment later, Frank appeared by her side, his wallet in his hands.

"What are you doing?"

"I'm giving her money."

She grasped his jacket sleeve. "Giving her money won't help if there's no place to sleep."

"What's your plan?" His helpless expression was annoyingly endearing.

She bit the bottom of her top lip. "We can invite her to come with us."

"With us?" He raised his brows.

"Yes, you and Roy too."

"You running a hotel?"

"No, but Mom has plenty of room."

He stared at her for a full minute before backing away. "That's ridiculous. You can't spring a carload of strangers on your mom. Especially on Christmas Eve."

Her mind made up, her determination strengthened. "It's the right thing to do because it *is* Christmas Eve. It's what Jesus would have done. It's what He wants me to do." She locked her gaze on his unswerving one, ready for his rebuttal.

He closed his eyes and took a deep breath. A second later Joan was surprised to hear his baritone voice quoting a familiar scripture. "'And she gave birth to her firstborn, a son. She wrapped him in cloths and placed him in a manger, because there was no room for him in the inn.'" His eyes softened. "Are you sure? That's a passel of people to deal with at once."

"Sure, I'm sure," she said. It was her mother she wasn't sure about.

"She's getting away!" Roy yelled through his half-opened window.

Joan turned to see the woman hurrying half a block away, garbage bag under one arm, cat dangling under the other. Mindful of the winter conditions, they rushed after her.

As they closed in on her, she shouted over her shoulder, "Leave me alone!"

Frank dropped his grip on Joan and charged ahead. He faced the woman with his palms toward her. "Wait, we just want to talk."

The woman drew her bag and cat close to her chest as if guarding them. "What do you want?"

"I want you to spend Christmas with us," Joan answered.

"What?" With her face scrunched up in disbelief, she roamed her gaze from Joan to Frank, to the SUV, and back again. Even the cat sent Joan a disgruntled look.

Joan took a cautious step forward. "Please. Call it good will or Christian charity or whatever you want, but somehow I've ended up with a carload of strangers and your presence will make our Christmas complete."

"What are you—a nut or a social worker?"

"Not a social worker." Joan's laugh felt cathartic. "Maybe a nut. We'll see. Do you have somewhere else to go?"

The woman licked her lips, drawing the cat's attention to them. It raised one paw and softly batted her mouth. She gazed down with tenderness. "It's okay, George, you go where I go." She placed his paw on her cheek and rubbed noses with him. "Isn't that right, Georgie? You and I are a team. That's right, we are," she crooned. Purring, George turned his head exposing his creamy throat to her face in a touching testament of trust.

Cold seeped through the seams of Joan's gloves, so she knew the woman's bare hands must be frigid. "Yes, we have room for George too. And if you don't want to come with us, at least let me buy you a cup of coffee. It looked like the new gas station was still open."

"Well, I'll take you up on the coffee."

As they arrived at the vehicle, Frank opened the driver's side rear door.

The woman peered inside. "There's no room. You want me to ride on the roof?"

Joan didn't blink at the woman's sass. "Sure, go ahead and climb up. You can't beat the view, but hang tight to the rails or you might roll off." The last thing she saw before she rounded the back of the SUV was the woman's mouth open in a perfect circle. Grinning, Joan moved the luggage to reveal the latch for the third seat. Once it was up, she called out, "Foster? Roy? How about you two sit back here?" She didn't need to ask twice.

They drove back to the highway in silence. At the gas station, Joan, Frank, and the woman got out, but the woman wouldn't go inside, saying George wasn't allowed.

A few minutes later, Joan and Frank returned and passed around coffee and hot chocolate. The woman stood off to the side trying to juggle her bag, cat, and coffee. Joan stood beside her door, hand on the latch. "Are you sure? You're more than welcome."

A yearning expression came over the woman's face. Her shoulders dropped as if in defeat, but finally she smiled. "You know, I really would."

Once more they hit the road with Joan mentally reciting... *and then there were six.* Well, seven if one counted George.

AFTER A QUICK INTRODUCTION ALL AROUND, MIRANDA practically pounced on the woman—who revealed her name was Dottie—digging for information about her circumstances.

"It was all different a year ago. Then George died—my husband George, not my cat. We never did have much savings, and between the medical bills and the funeral costs, by the time his estate was settled there wasn't much left."

As Dottie continued her story, Joan thought of Mom's circumstances. Whenever she had asked financial questions, Mom had waved them away as if they weren't important. Joan didn't know anything about her state of affairs. Before she left, she'd get Mom alone and press the issue. But the house would be full of people. Strangers. *Oh, Lord, help me.*

They turned off the highway and entered Fiska.

Joan slowed the SUV as she made the last few turns to her childhood home. She pulled into the driveway, emotionally drained, caught off guard by the brilliance of the Christmas lights embellishing the veranda railing and gingerbread trim. In the parlor window, a brightly decorated tree stood sentinel beside Mom's silhouette. She waved and was gone.

No one in the SUV moved.

"Is this it?" squeaked Roy.

The front door opened and Mom stepped under the veranda light, closing the door behind her. Looking like a meadowlark in her yellow sweater with the black trim, she crossed her arms to ward off the cold.

Joan's gaze drank in the beauty of the sight. "Yes, this is home."

Mom beamed at Joan as she left the safety of her vehicle and ran up the path to greet her, but halfway there the sounds of doors opening and closing drew Mom's attention. "Joanie?"

"Mom—"

"I see a man." Mom beamed down at her. "Have you found someone special?"

Joan ran up the steps. "Frank's not—"

Craning forward, Mom squinted. "Oh, he has a wife."

Joan hugged her. "No, that's my friend Miranda, but—"

Mom shifted to see around Joan. "Is he divorced? I see one—no, two kids."

"No, Mom, he's widowed, but—" Joan blocked Mom's view, but she craned around the other way.

"And he brought his mother?" Mom stepped back with a deadpan expression. "You brought home a ready-made family?"

"No, I didn't, but would it be so bad if I did?" Hearing footsteps coming up the path, she locked eyes with her mother. "I don't know why, but God put these special strangers in my path and I couldn't turn them away."

Mom held her gaze as if trying to read something in her words. "You brought strangers to my home for Christmas?"

Ready for anything, Joan nodded.

She pulled Joan into another hug and whispered in her ear, "Just like your dad would have done." Turning a teary smile on the crowd of strangers waiting quietly at the bottom of the steps, she opened her arms and greeted them. "Merry Christmas! And welcome to our home. There's a roaring fire and hot apple cider waiting for you in the parlor."

Roy bounded up the steps. "A real fire? Dad! This is going to be the best Christmas ever!"

Frank swallowed. "Please forgive Roy. We had planned to watch the fireplace channel in a motel room tonight." He stretched out his hand and gave hers a firm shake. "Frank Larson at your service, ma'am. I'll tell you straight...your daughter's beauty shines inside as well as out."

"*Hmm*," Mom murmured as he faded back down the steps, dragging Joan's gaze after him.

Miranda approached. "Mom, this is my friend, Miranda. She planned on spending Christmas at her grandma's but, well, it's a long story."

Mom gently pushed Miranda toward the door. "Why don't you go in and call her? The phone's in the hall and I'm on a plan, so don't worry about the long-distance charges."

Miranda flashed Joan a grin as she passed. Behind her, Foster helped Dottie and George up the steps. Before Joan could figure out how to introduce the runaway, Foster stepped forward.

"I'm Sarah. Could I use your phone after Miranda? I'd like to call my foster parents."

Joan stood in amazement, humbled by the turn of events. How could she have doubted?

With Sarah inside, Dottie set down her bag and turned to Joan's mom. "I apologize for coming in such a state—"

"Dottie?" Mom pulled her under the porch light and scrutinized her face. "Dottie Olson, is that really you?"

It was Dottie's turn to stare. "Yes, but—"

"Oh." Mom drew Dottie into a bear hug that made George meow in a disapproving manner. "I'm Janet Brody. Well, I'm Janet Rigler now, but I was Janet Brody back then. I always wondered what happened to you." She turned to Joan, more animated than she'd been since their arrival. "Oh, Joanie, I haven't seen Dottie since she left high school in the middle of our final year. And here I've left you standing out in the cold. Come in, come in..."

AS THEIR GUESTS WERE MAKING THEMSELVES comfortable, Joan wandered through the house, noting the familiar holiday greenery displayed exactly as it had been when Dad was alive. Even the dining room table was set with the poinsettia-patterned china. But why so many place settings? She hadn't phoned to say there would be five extra people for dinner on Christmas Day. Well, six if one counted George. Add herself and Mom, and that made eight. Staring at the table, she tapped her mug.

Mom wrapped her arm around Joan's waist. "Thank you for my Christmas present."

"You never cease to amaze me." Joan gestured to the table. "How did you know I was bringing guests?"

"I didn't." She sighed. "I decided to set the table for the two of us so I wouldn't think about you driving out there all alone. As I worked, I remembered one time when your Aunt Belle showed up unannounced at the most inconvenient time and wouldn't leave. She was so demanding back then and I couldn't deal with it that weekend. I'm afraid I turned into a screaming banshee. Oh, but you were too young to remember that."

Joan didn't correct her.

"Anyway," Mom continued, "by the time I got through confessing my wrong and asking Jesus for a chance to atone for my selfishness, I realized I'd put the complete set out, water glasses and all. It looked too pretty to put away. And now it's ready for tomorrow." She kissed Joan's cheek. "Thanks to you, we have a house full of guests to entertain. Come on, they're waiting." With a radiant smile, she was gone.

Joan gave the dining room a final look of wonder before turning off the light. She entered the hall as Sarah set the phone down.

With a shy smile, Sarah said, "My foster-mom is going to call tomorrow morning. Can I stay until you go back?"

"You bet," Joan said. She praised God for putting the runaway at the truck stop at the perfect moment for them to meet.

As she neared the parlor, she heard the familiar strains of a favorite carol. "Join me!" Mom called out, as her fingers flew over the keys of the old family upright. "Hark! The her-ald..."

Joan stopped in the wide arched doorway. Roy was already asleep on the couch, George curled close to his chest. Sarah and Miranda sat on the floor near the crackling hearth. Dottie stood beside the piano, her lovely voice accompanying Mom's playing.

She rested her head against the door frame. All she'd wanted this Christmas was for Mom not to be alone. God heard her prayer and sent her a-wassailing, gathering strangers along the way and bringing them together as friends to share a wassail bowl of memories.

Frank strolled over, a mug in one hand. He glanced up at the mistletoe above Joan, then grinned with a wink before gathering her into a hug. "Thank you," he said, his eyes warm. "This is...wonderful, just what Roy and I needed. How can I ever thank you?"

"It wasn't me, Frank. God did it. I was just the driver."

THE MEMORY SHOP

Carla Olson Gade

Arthur Preble looked up from his 1915 cast metal cash register as the jingle of antique bells announced a customer entering his memorabilia shop. A gust of wind followed the middle-aged man inside, along with a few dried leaves. Winter was in the air, and soon Christmas would be as well. At least it ought to be. Arthur was behind in getting his decorations up for Main Street's first Christmas since the downtown revitalization project.

"Ah!" The man looked up at the tarnished shopkeeper bells dangling over the door. "Just as I remember."

Arthur shut the drawer of the ornate cash register—affectionately named Old 1915—and turned to look at the clock on the wall behind him. Five minutes past four. He really should skedaddle.

The customer swept an affectionate look around at the tables and shelves clustered with all manner of vintage items, and a smile emerged on his face. He looked back at Arthur. "The memory shop. I know it's Memory Lane, but that's what we always called it." The familiar-looking fellow stuffed his gloves into the pockets of his down vest. "You are open, aren't you, Mr. Preble?"

Arthur pushed his glasses over the bridge of his nose. "Aren't you Will, Ted Stanton's son? Don't you live in Oskaloosa?"

"I am and I do." Will offered a lopsided smile, reminding Arthur of the quirky boy he once knew.

"Then you betcha I'm still open." Arthur grinned and moved out from behind the counter to shake Will's hand.

"You sure, Mr. Preble?" Will asked.

"Why, sure I'm sure. I'd hate to have you go back empty-handed. You've come quite a distance. I'm flattered," Arthur teased. "Just watch your step. I put some boxes of Christmas decorations and whatnot out on the floor to put up in the morning."

Will glanced around. "No problem."

"So what's the occasion, Will? Don't tell me your father is having another birthday? Because if he is, that makes me another year older too." Arthur tucked his chin in, lifting his white eyebrows.

"That's right," Will said. "You both have Christmas Eve birthdays. He used to mention that every now and then. Every Christmas Eve, in fact. He'd say, 'Imagine that, Arthur Preble and I, both from the class of 1957, born on the same day, same year.'"

"Yes, and there were only thirty-four students in our class," Arthur said.

Will joined him in saying, "Fifteen boys and nineteen girls."

"So you've heard." Arthur chuckled. "And we married two of the prettiest girls among them."

"He'd say that too," Will said.

Will picked up a mug with his high school insignia. "How *is* Mrs. Preble?"

"Ah...she's just as pretty as ever, she is," Arthur said, not wanting to elaborate.

"She was my favorite English teacher. I've never forgotten her penchant for memorization." Will set the mug down.

Hmm. Arthur pressed his lips together. "And your mother, Will?"

"She's doing better after her stroke last year. She sent me in to pick up some things for Dad's party to remind him of his youth here in good ol' Woodbine, Iowa."

"He'll get a kick out of that, the old fossil," Arthur said.

Will cocked his head and offered an admiring smile. "Why, you and Dad are two of the most young-at-heart fellows I know."

"I knew there was some reason I liked you, young man." Arthur chuckled and shook his head.

As they talked, Will browsed tables laden with mementos and trinkets popular in days gone by. He gazed up at a 1945 Rodgers and Hammerstein *State Fair* musical poster. "Hey, would you happen to have that film on VHS?"

"VHS? He won't give up his old player, eh?"

"We are talking about my dad, Mr. Preble. He just keeps fixing it when it jams." Will shrugged. "No doubt you'll be busy with your own family on Christmas Eve, but you and Mrs. Preble are always welcome to join us."

The words of Will's polite invitation floated toward Arthur with the bite of an approaching snowstorm. Another birthday, another Christmas with his skeleton of a family. Sure, his wife would be by his side and her sister and brother-in-law would drop by after spending time with their own family, complete with the laughter of grandchildren. What was Christmastime to him but a season to be lonely? And to remember. So many beautiful memories, along with some painful regrets.

Was that all he had left? What chance was there now to make new memories? He shook himself from his reverie and smiled.

"Well now, I appreciate that. But I have the shop and everything. Pert' sure I'll have some last-minute customers." Arthur scrunched his mouth to the side while thinking. "I'll tell you what. Let me pick out something for Ted and tell him it's from his birthday buddy." And he knew just the thing. Arthur ambled over to the counter and slid open the glass door of the display cabinet. He placed a shiny blue model car on the counter. "A 1951 Buick Riviera. Like the one we both had back in our youth."

Will walked toward him nodding, and a mischievous smirk appeared.

"It was Ted's first car. Mine too...after I bought it from him." Arthur slowly shook his head. "Purred like a kitten."

"Really?"

"Not at all!" Arthur laughed. "You could hear it coming half a mile away. But it sure was sweet."

Will gestured toward the model. "May I?"

"By all means." Arthur handed the car to Will. "They don't make 'em like that anymore."

Will inspected the plastic vehicle. "Don't you want to keep this? They're your memories too."

"Yes, and good ones. Although I can think of a time or two that your father and I got into trouble in this thing."

Will raised an eyebrow. "Do tell."

"Oh no. You've got to ask your old man about that yourself." Arthur took in a deep breath and his thoughts drifted away. A sudden wave of dark dizziness came over him and he stumbled back.

Will reached across the counter to steady him. "You okay?"

Arthur took a hanky out of his pocket and wiped perspiration from his brow. "I'm fine. Just lost my balance."

Will gazed at Arthur with concern. "Are you sure?"

Arthur nodded and took a sip of water from a Dixie cup sitting by the register.

As Arthur plopped down on his stool, Will tentatively resumed the conversation. "Did you put this model together?"

"I did. But I've enjoyed it. Now it's time to pass it along," said Arthur, feeling steadier on his feet.

"You don't want to give it to Hal or his kid?" Will asked.

Arthur's chest constricted. He didn't see that coming. "No need."

Will hiked his chin, and Arthur could see the question in his eyes. Did he have any idea that Arthur hadn't spoken to his son in years?

Arthur shook his head. "Take it to your father. A gift from me for our mutual birthday."

"If you're sure. I appreciate it." Will looked over Arthur's shoulder toward the clock behind him. "It's getting late, and I've imposed on you long enough. I'm not headed back until later tomorrow, so I'll come back in the morning. I can give you a hand with those Christmas decorations."

"I'll take you up on your offer," Arthur said. "Besides, I have the missing headlight for this car around here somewhere...How about I fix it up and you can take it with you then?"

Will retrieved his gloves from his vest pockets and readied to go out into the cold. "See you in the morning."

ARTHUR GLANCED OUT THE LARGE STOREFRONT window, watching as people passed by. A woman pushing a stroller, a man on a bike, a couple of women crossing the street toward the café. A police cruiser drove by and the officer waved at Arthur as he passed, followed by the daily delivery truck that stopped at Main Street's new restaurant. A laborer set up a ladder near one of the old-fashioned street lamps that the town recently had invested in and began the task of adjusting a drooping Christmas wreath mounted there.

Woodbine's revitalized Main Street made Arthur's heart swell with pride. He'd been one of the last holdouts in the formerly dormant downtown for years. As one of the small Midwestern town's mainstays, Memory Lane wasn't just a shop; it was an institution, an icon. Besides, he wasn't in it to make money; he'd spent plenty of time doing that as a successful aeronautical inventor, allowing him to retire early.

For the past seventeen years Arthur's mission had been to make and preserve memories, help keep up the morale of the town. But he felt the sting of irony that, despite the wealth of memories overflowing the shelves of his shop, they were all he had. He certainly wasn't making any memories with his own son. The two men were estranged, and Arthur still didn't know why after all these years, despite his efforts to reach out and close the gulf between them.

The door bells jingled, snapping Arthur to attention. "Edna! Pastor Tom! How nice of you to stop by. I'm afraid I'm behind in my Christmas decorating. It looks like the rest of the shops on Main Street are way ahead of me."

"'Morning, Arthur. It's fantastic to see what is happening to this town! Could it be returning to its glory days?" The minister tilted his head with enthusiasm. "I hear they're planning a Christmas parade for next year. Trinity Church's youth should enter a float."

Arthur clapped his hands together. "Then count on Memory Lane to sponsor it."

"Marvelous!" Pastor Tom exclaimed. "Don't you think so Edna? A parade!"

"A parade?" Edna turned and headed toward the front door. "Where?"

The minister gently redirected her. "It'll be next year. We shall have a parade next year."

"Oh, for Independence Day? Will we have fireworks too? That's a wonderful idea." Edna turned to Arthur. "Do you sell fireworks here?"

"No. But we do have some other things you might like to see." Arthur placed his hand on Edna's back. "Come this way, dear."

As Edna turned, she caught a glimpse of the '51 Buick model car he'd repaired earlier, sitting on the counter for Will. Arthur watched her with anticipation. Would his wife recognize the little vehicle that she'd seen so many times before? Arthur never knew what to expect when his wife came to the shop and saw things out of their normal context. Yet he was grateful that Pastor Tom brought her during their weekly coffee outing. If it wasn't for Pastor, the day care center, and Edna's sister, he didn't know how he would manage. They'd all convinced him that keeping the shop would be a good outlet for him, but it was a hard choice to make. She looked clear eyed this morning, attentive.

Would she recognize him today?

The question broke his heart.

Edna studied the car model with the wistful touch of her slender hand. A hand Arthur longed to hold in a meaningful way, and if he had his druthers, he would. But in this setting it would be impossible. How lovely Edna still was. Though her youth had faded, her beauty had not.

Edna picked up the car. Would she remember?

"A 1951 Buick." Her eyes darted toward Arthur and back again at the model. "My first date was in a blue Buick like this." She looked at Arthur again and winked.

Arthur blushed, averting his eyes from Pastor Tom. He stifled a laugh. He'd never known her to wink before.

"Have we met?" she asked. "I had a boyfriend named Arthur once." Edna looked around. "Where is my purse? Did someone take it? I must go pay the taxi before he leaves."

Pastor Tom spoke in an even tone. "No need, Edna. We're going to take my car."

"Oh, do you have a Buick too?" Edna asked. "I hope it's blue. Have you found my purse yet, Tom?"

Arthur glanced at Edna, noting her purse dangling from her wrist. Arthur's eyes connected with the pastor's. This man—friend to so many—was a godsend in Edna's life. And in his.

"Your purse is right there, Edna," the minister said.

"Oh, good. I thought I left it at home." Edna smiled at Arthur. "May I pay for the little car now? I'd like to give it to my husband for Christmas."

Arthur's voice caught in his throat. As he looked into Edna's searching eyes, the words erupted from his mouth. "You betcha."

Now he was in a pickle.

Arthur managed to put up a few strings of garland and spray a little fake snow into the corners of the plate glass windows after Edna and Pastor Tom left the store. As he rummaged through the carton of old Christmas decorations, Will came in. What would he tell Will about the model car for Ted?

"'Morning, Mr. Preble. It's beginning to look a lot like Christmas!" Will said, gesturing toward the storefront windows.

"It's a start."

"Let's see if we can remedy that. Sorry I'm running a little late this morning. Had some errands to take care of before I head back to Oskaloosa." Will handed

Arthur a paper cup. "Coffee? Grabbed it from the café across the street. Nice to see business picking up downtown. Reminds me of when I was a kid."

Arthur nodded and took a sip of the coffee, his elbow extended midair as he tilted it back. "This was sure nice of you, Will."

"How's she doing today?"

She? Does he know about Edna? The steaming liquid slipped down Arthur's throat the wrong way. Will came rushing over to him and slapped him on the back as Arthur sputtered and spurted away. Arthur held his hand up. "I'm good, thanks."

"So, how's she doing?" Will looked over at the display counter by the cash register at the bright-blue model car. "Did you get the headlight glued back on to the Buick?"

"Fit right on." Arthur plodded toward the counter and Will followed.

"My dad's going to love it."

"Uh, about that." Arthur rubbed his jaw. "There's something I need to explain."

COULD YOU BEAT THAT? THE APPLE DIDN'T FALL FAR from the tree. Will Stanton had the same good nature as his father. When Arthur divulged the situation about Edna purchasing the model car and how he didn't have the heart to prevent it, Will was more than accepting. He said the gift was in the thought, and he appreciated the idea. Will would look for a similar model on one of those Internet auction Web sites and request a Christmas delivery.

After helping Arthur get the Christmas tree set up, some trimmings around the shop, and a string of C7 ceramic-coated holiday lightbulbs around the windows, Memory Lane looked downright magical. He hoped his patrons would feel the same. He didn't mind if they only came in to browse. The important thing is that they left feeling good and could pass some of that joy around. He hoped Ted would enjoy some of the nostalgic pieces his son selected for him. They'd be good conversation items. Help him reminisce and share his story with his family and friends. That's what was important.

Arthur sat on his stool by the cash register. He could tell he wasn't getting any younger either. The morning had pert' near done him in. Maybe this woozy feeling meant it was time for lunch. He glanced up at the clock. Sure enough. Twelve noon.

By the time he unwrapped his tuna sandwich and flipped the tab off his can of pop, the bells over the door jingled, welcoming more customers. Lois and Linda Wilson, Woodbine's resident crafters, sporting matching homemade Christmas sweaters.

"Hello, Mr. Preble. The place looks enchanting!" Linda exclaimed.

"Between the Applefest in September and last weekend's Christmas fair, we're clean out of C7s." Lois beamed. "We've sold twenty-six holiday lightbulb wreaths and have orders for a dozen more."

"You're in luck, ladies. There are a couple of boxes in the back aisle with your name on them." Those gals were industrious, he'd give them that.

"You are a dear, Arthur Preble." Lois smiled and scurried after her sister.

Arthur took a bite of his sandwich. He might as well take his lunch. The gals were sure to browse around for another three-quarters of an hour or so.

Lois tugged her rumpled sweater over her ample hips. "Are you sure you won't sell us the lights in the window?"

Linda's chin dipped. "Now, Lois, leave the good man a little something to draw attention to his store-front. After all, Memory Lane is the inspiration behind the Main Street renaissance."

Lois replied in a stage whisper. "He still has that adorable corrugated cardboard fireplace and aluminum Christmas tree in the window. Not to mention the rotating colored lights shining on it."

"You just did, dear," said Linda.

"I promise to give you a call when we get some more C7s in stock," Arthur said, sliding their selections toward Old 1915.

"Mr. Preble," Lois said, "you are the gem of Woodbine."

How he loved the folks of Woodbine. "Let's ring up your purchases and I'll help you out with these boxes."

"Oh, Mr. Preble. I bet you say that to all the girls," Linda teased.

Lois giggled. "Especially his customers."

"Oh! We almost forgot!" Linda pressed a small wrapped package into his the palm. "Just a little something we made for you this Christmas."

ARTHUR CLIPPED A SHORT STRING OF BUBBLING LIGHTS to the Christmas tree stationed in the center of the memory shop. Funny how he'd come to think of Memory Lane that way over the years, just as his patrons did. As he fidgeted with the lights he thought again of the Wilson sisters, and the little reindeer ornament they'd given him earlier, made from one of the many C7 lightbulbs they'd purchased from him recently. He'd give it to Edna tonight after picking her up from adult day care. She could put in on their own small Christmas tree at home.

Arthur looked toward the window and noted the sky growing dim. The streetlights blinked on then, illuminating large, fluffy flakes floating down from the sky. *Lord, thank You for the little things that remind me You are still there.*

He reached into the box of vintage ornaments to replace some that had been sold. Arthur grabbed a colorful one from the corner—a cute little boy on skis. Tears pooled in his eyes as if from nowhere. No—from somewhere deep within. As Arthur stared at the plastic ornament, the face seemed to transform into the features of his own little boy, Hal, now a grown man with a son of his own. How Hal loved to ski! Arthur remembered clear as day when he took Hal up the hill behind the school to teach him. Had Hal taught his own boy to ski and sled too?

Pain and regret bounded over him like an avalanche. If only...

It was no use. He'd done all he could. Or had he? Arthur's head throbbed and his limbs felt week. The ornament he was clutching slipped from his grasp. He bent to pick it up and another wave of dizziness swept over him. Arthur extended his hand toward the only thing within his reach. Down he went, along with the Christmas tree in the center of his store.

"DAD? DAD!"

Arthur attempted to shake the haziness away, but his mind continued to play the cruel trick on him, the image of his son kneeling in front of him.

"Dad." A firm grip helped Arthur to his feet. "You had me scared there for a minute."

Arthur focused. *Hal!* His eyes hadn't betrayed him.

"Hal. How did you get here?" Arthur asked.

"The better question is, 'How did you get there?'" Hal pointed to the floor.

"Not really sure, a little light-headed, I guess." Arthur pressed his palm against his forehead. "I dropped an ornament..."

"This?" A boy of about eight handed Arthur the little skier ornament.

"Yep, that's the one." Arthur accepted the ornament but continued to gaze into the boy's big brown eyes.

Hal looked at the boy in amazement. "How did you know which one?"

The boy—the spitting image of a young Hal—shrugged. "All the others are broken."

Arthur surveyed the disaster of the fallen Christmas tree, with scattered trimmings and shards of broken ornaments everywhere.

"C'mon, stand over there, Artie. I don't want you getting hurt too, like your grandfather." Hal took

Arthur by the arm and brought him over to a bench by the counter. "Are you all right, Dad? Have you been having dizzy spells for long?"

"Ah, every now and then. Nothing to worry about."

"What other symptoms do you have?" Hal cupped his hands around Arthur's head, feeling for bumps, while his son hovered behind him. "Did you bang your head when you fell?"

"I suppose I banged it, but you know how hard-headed I am. I don't think it broke anything." Arthur warded off Hal's hands.

"Hardheaded? Don't get me started." Hal snorted. "Let's get you to the ER."

"No need. What I'd really like to do is meet my grandson." Arthur tilted his head and grinned at the boy—the boy he had longed to know since the child's birth. Hal had sent him a few pictures, but they had stopped after a short time. And he and Edna had sent something for Artie's birthday each year . . . But Arthur had supposed it was too much to ask to ever meet the child in person, fanning the flames of hurt. But now, here he was. His namesake. Arthur felt unexpectedly nervous.

Hal put his hands around his son's shoulders. "Dad. This is Artie." Hal blew out a little breath. "Your grandson."

Arthur reached his hand out toward the boy, but Artie stood back. Arthur looked up at Hal and asked, half-teasing, "Haven't you taught him how to shake?"

"Of course. Go ahead, Artie."

Artie stepped forward and took Arthur's hand. A silly grin appeared on the boy's face. "Hi, Granddad."

"So that's what you are going to call me...Granddad." Arthur smiled. "That'll do."

Arthur stood and looked over at the mess in the center of the store. "I'd better get that cleaned up."

"Not before you go to the ER to get checked," Hal insisted, his brow creased with worry, making him look older than Arthur recalled. But then again, it had been nearly eight years since he'd last seen his son.

"Hal, I don't need to go to the hospital." Arthur's brow wrinkled.

"Let's give your doctor a call and see what he says." Hal's tone was serious. "I haven't come here to argue with you."

"Then why *are* you here, son?"

Hal's jaw grew taut. He glanced at Artie, who had wandered to the back of the store to investigate the curiosities. "I'm here to ask your forgiveness."

Arthur swallowed hard. "Will you accept it? I offered it long ago when I offered my own apologies for all the times we disagreed. We can't take back all that's been said. Everything we left unsaid."

"It wasn't about that, Dad." Hal shuffled his feet. "It was…"

"What?" Arthur pinched his brow, then his eyes widened in realization. "We wondered why she always returned Artie's gifts. Were they never enough?"

"Dad, nothing was enough for her. She's emotionally bankrupt." Hal sent a quick glance toward Artie, happily occupied with the Matchbox car collection. He spoke in a low voice. "It was either her and Artie, or you and mom. It was an impossible choice." Deep sorrow shadowed Hal's face. "I finally stopped playing her games, Dad. So here I am."

"And Artie?"

"I have primary custody. I'm moving back to Woodbine."

Arthur glanced at his grandson with an overwhelming urge to love and protect him. His heart also broke for his son and the heartache he had endured. Strange how compassion now overrode the anger and hurt he'd once felt. Arthur reached out to Hal. "Oh, son."

As father and son embraced, the release of forgiveness washed over them. Arthur patted Hal on his back as the pair glanced over at Artie, still occupied with the Matchbox cars. "He's a fine boy, Hal. I can see that. Bright. Well-behaved."

"I can't wait for Mother to get to know him." Hal swiped at a tear trailing down his cheek. "I hope she can forget all the suffering I have caused her."

"Hal. About your mother..."

"DAD." HAL TOOK THE BROOM FROM ARTHUR'S GRIP. "Dr. Hayden said you'll need to take it slow until your low-blood-pressure medication is adjusted. If you don't allow me to help you for the next few days until Christmas Eve, I'll have to tie you up and put you in the storeroom."

Arthur scowled. "You wouldn't."

"Don't tempt me." Hal feigned a reciprocal scowl.

Artie snuck up behind Hal with a scowl of his own. "Dad, stop being mean to Granddad. He's just an old man."

"Who are you calling old, young man?" Arthur teased, and tweaked Artie's nose.

"Are you as old as Santa Claus?" his grandson asked.

Hal chimed in. "No. But he's going to be. His birthday is on Christmas Eve, don't you know."

"Really? And Jesus' birthday is on Christmas." Artie seemed impressed.

Arthur ruffled Artie's hair. "Thanks for helping your father get that Christmas tree cleaned up. Now we need to decorate it again." Arthur was still in awe at the turn of events. "How about it? Would you like to help trim that tree?"

Artie grabbed a knee-hugger elf from a bin. "Can I put him on it?"

"You betcha," Arthur said.

His grandson pointed to the small boxes of glass ornaments. "What about these?"

Hal cocked his head. "Why don't you put these satin ones on instead? They're the special ones. I remember we had some like that on our tree when I grew up. Then we'll put on some of this tinsel and top it with this rather crinkled-looking foil star."

Hal looked at Arthur. "I can't believe this stuff is still around. Totally changes the look of a Christmas tree."

Hal picked up a vintage box of Shiny-Brite ornaments. "Isn't mercury glass toxic? That could be a liability for Memory Lane."

"There's no mercury in them. It's only a silvery substance that looks like mercury." Arthur chuckled. "If it was, the world would've gone mad by now."

"Well, maybe that explains it," Hal said with a laugh. He hung a lantern-shaped ornament on an upper branch. "So, Dad, has the Main Street revitalization been good for business?"

"Sure has. The new restaurant came in and bought a slew of Woodbine memorabilia to decorate their dining

room. Some of the local college students come in some-
times to get 'retro' décor for their dorms," Arthur said.

Hal nodded with interest.

"We've had an incredible boon this holiday season.
Which reminds me, Will Stanton was in a little while
back."

"So I heard."

Arthur narrowed his eyes. "Oh?"

"He called me."

Arthur's brow rose. "I wondered if he might have."

"Dad, I wish I'd known sooner about Mom. There's
so much I regret."

"I've realized that regret is a dangerous thing, son.
Some folks hold on to it like one of these precious mementos." Arthur motioned around the store. "It can spur
us to change, or we can dwell in it and it will destroy us."

Hal nodded. "I'm glad we chose the former."

"You betcha!" Arthur said with a broad grin.

Until Christmas Eve day, customers continued
to trickle into Memory Lane, including the Wilson
sisters, who came bearing a gift of their special
Christmas loaf. By midafternoon, Arthur began to
think about closing shop. Edna's day care Christmas
party would be ending and he expected Pastor Tom
to bring her by the store before he went back to the
church to prepare for the Christmas Eve service.

"I'm beginning to feel more like my old self again," Arthur told his son. "Pert' sure that's a good thing."

"Indeed it is, since today's your birthday and tomorrow's Christmas!" Hal said as he wiped a glass display case.

Artie handed his grandfather a handmade card. "Happy birthday, Granddad."

Arthur opened the envelope. "Thank you, Artie. I will treasure this."

"Like you do all the things in your store?" Artie asked.

Arthur stooped beside his grandson. "Those aren't the things I treasure. It's people I treasure most. Like you, your father, and your grandmother—whom you'll get to meet soon." Although Hal and Artie were staying with Edna's sister and husband, only Hal had been to see his mother. They hadn't wanted it all to be too much for her to take in at once.

Before long, the bustle of Main Street quieted as townsfolk went their way to begin their Christmas celebrations. Arthur peeked out the front windows, enjoying the peaceful moment before he went over to say good night to Old 1915.

The brass bells announced Edna and Pastor Tom. Edna was immediately drawn to the little boy who looked so much like her son had as a child. Hal introduced Artie to his grandmother, and although somewhat confused, she seemed to take him at his word. But she also looked to Arthur for a nod of affirmation, and Arthur's heart overflowed with gratitude at the presence of his family together again.

As Artie played with an old train set that he and Hal had put up around the Christmas tree display, Edna asked Artie questions and told him about another little boy who once had a similar train set as a child. Artie was so accepting, even when his grandmother repeated the same stories over again. Hal watched, obviously moved by the interaction between his mother and his son. There would be challenges, Arthur knew, but his reunited family would face them together.

When they were ready to go, Hal helped his mother on with her faux fur coat and walked her to the door into the vibrant lights of Woodbine's Main Street. Artie tugged on Arthur's jacket sleeve and looked up at him with shining eyes. "Merry Christmas, Granddad!"

"Merry Christmas, Artie." The antique bells on the door jangled as the family exited Memory Lane, and Arthur glanced back, thinking of the host of memories lingering behind him in the shop. They'd still be there when he returned after Christmas, but they were nothing compared to the joy bubbling up inside him as he took his grandson's hand. "Let's go home, Artie. We have some new memories to make."

A Bloom in Winter

Ann Mateer

Alicia wiped dust from the green top of a clear plastic tub, then sat back on her heels, her knees creaking with the effort. How could one feel both twenty-five and seventy-five at the same moment?

She pushed to her feet and surveyed the collection of boxes before her. A lifetime of Christmas decorations confined to such a small space. But then, she'd given away so many things after Fred died three years ago.

Who would she decorate for now? Her kids and grandkids lived so far away. And the university students who'd clustered around Dr. Fred for so many years had no reason to stop by to see her now that she was all alone. They'd come for his witty conversation and his expertise in the field of engineering. She'd only been the wife—the person who served the food they devoured, the one they thanked on the way out for filling their usually empty stomachs. A student's budget, you know.

Oh, did she know! It seemed like yesterday, Fred working frantically on his dissertation while she schlepped to her waitressing job at the diner in all kinds of weather. They'd had good times on pennies a day. And their diligence had led to even brighter memories in times of plenty. At least until his heart stopped beating and he left her alone in this big old house.

She popped the top from one tub. A porcelain angel stared up at her through protective plastic packaging. "I bring you good tidings of great joy!" its banner declared. Alicia lifted the tree-topper from its resting place and set it on the table beside the sofa before glancing toward the back of the house.

Maybe taking in a boarder had been a good idea after all. A reason to dust off old memories, old habits. Get back to living. She knew plenty of students were interested in the cheap rent she offered, but why she'd chosen Maggie from all the engineering graduate student applications she'd received, she couldn't quite say.

She lifted five stockings, her own handiwork, from the box. She ran her wrinkled fingers over the neat needlepoint spelling out her children's names, then Fred's, before returning the stockings to the plastic bin. Better to pick up a couple of those generic red ones with the white fuzz on top. One for her, one for Maggie. It would be less hurtful to see new ones hanging from the pine mantel that framed the stone fireplace.

The mantel.

With renewed vigor, she dug through one tub, then another, finally happening upon the mahogany nativity set Jenny had brought home from her first trip to Ghana, before she moved there permanently to run a rescue mission for young girls.

One tear slipped down the side of Alicia's face, but not so much for missing her girl as for gratitude that she'd raised a woman who dedicated her life to pleasing the Lord. As did her sons Marcus and Daniel, each committing their vocation to the Lord as they'd seen their father do.

And that, she realized, was why she'd chosen Maggie over all the others. Alicia had also long ago committed her vocation—wife and mother—to the Lord as her ministry, but without a husband or children to care for, she'd fallen into disuse. Her fault, not God's, she realized. When dear Dr. Whitman—once Fred's student, now chairman of the engineering department—suggested taking in a student or two, she'd hesitated. Until she met Maggie. If she'd ever known anything in her seventy-five years on this earth, she knew that girl needed a friend.

A key jiggled in the back door before it swung open, bringing a blast of winter air with it. Alicia hurried to the kitchen and poured hot coffee into a tall mug. She set it on the kitchen table as Maggie unwound a scarf from her face and head.

"Something to warm you up," Alicia said.

Maggie blinked her almond-shaped eyes as if Alicia had spoken Russian instead of English. Even after almost five months of living in this house, kindness still seemed to mystify the girl.

"Go on. I'll take your things."

Alicia helped Maggie shrug out of her coat, then carried it to the closet. When she returned to the kitchen, Maggie sat at the table, her mocha-colored hands wrapped around the ceramic cup.

"Did your classes go well today?" Alicia asked.

Maggie nodded, sipped.

Alicia poured herself some coffee and sat across from the girl, studying her delicate features framed by black corkscrew curls. She wondered again at the girl's heritage. And at her name. Maggie—short for Margaret, Alicia assumed.

"Finals start soon?"

"Yes, ma'am. Next week for undergrads. I have a final project due Friday."

"After that, you'll have a nice long break from studying." Alicia reached across and patted Maggie's hand.

The girl startled, wide eyes staring at the place where their skin met, then lifting to Alicia's face. Wariness radiated from Maggie's expression. Alicia pulled her hand back, remembering Jenny's description of some of the girls she'd worked with, the ones who took longer to trust that her motive for caring was their well-being alone. How could a girl with that kind of emotional fragility have made it as a PhD candidate at one of the most prestigious engineering schools in the country?

"Oh! I made cranberry pumpkin bread." Alicia hopped up, unwrapped a plate of sliced bread, and stuck it in the microwave. "I always prefer it warm."

When the bell dinged, Alicia returned to the table. Maggie gave her a small smile before sliding a slice to her napkin, pinching off the corner and popping it in her mouth. An expression of delight flashed across the girl's face, then disappeared.

Alicia leaned against the back of the chair, her fingers looped around the handle of her mug as a prayer for wisdom whispered through her head. A desire to know when to talk, when to stay silent. This, she decided, was a moment to push. "You haven't mentioned any holiday plans. Are you going home for Christmas?"

Maggie's chin dropped. She stared into her coffee, but not before Alicia had witnessed the lightning flicker of fear in her eyes.

"I don't—" Maggie glanced away, her jaw tightening and releasing before she heaved out a big breath. "I'll be here, if that's okay with you."

Alicia waited a moment, hoping Maggie would say more. When she didn't, Alicia broke the awkwardness by gathering up the pumpkin bread and their empty coffee cups and carrying them to the counter, not speaking again until her back was turned to her boarder. "That's perfectly fine with me. In fact, I'll be happy to have the company. My boys will spend Christmas with their own families, and, of course, my daughter is still in Africa."

"You won't go visit your kids?" A tentative question, but it sparked a smile on Alicia's lips. One which she erased before she turned to face Maggie again.

Alicia crossed her arms and leaned back against the sink. "They invited me, of course. But I decided I need Christmas here this year, in my own home. It might be the last time."

"Last time?" Maggie's gaze raced from one end of the room to the other, as if seeking some imperfection that would indicate the structural integrity of the house had been compromised.

Alicia laughed. "I've thought about selling the old place. It's too much for just me. But I hadn't the heart to let it go before now. Fred and I lived here—happily—for over thirty years. You don't just give up a place where the love of your life meets you around every corner."

Maggie ducked her head and muttered, "I suppose not."

"So I've decided if this Christmas is the last one here, I'd like to do it up right. The way I used to, when Fred brought hordes of students through our door for us to feed and fuss over." She swept her hand toward the living room. "I spent all day carrying Christmas decorations up from the basement."

Maggie leaned over to peek through the doorway leading to the living room. "You'd go to all that trouble just for the two of us? What if I'd said I had plans?"

Alicia shrugged. "I'd have done it anyway. Just for me. To remind me again of the joy of Christmas, the blessing of the Christ child born in a manger."

Maggie's mouth twisted into a smirk.

"You don't believe in that part of Christmas, do you?" Alicia asked.

Maggie stood and slid her messenger bag onto one shoulder. "No, ma'am. I don't. If you want to know the truth, I don't believe in any part of Christmas at all. It's just another day to me. But you decorate all you like. I have to study."

MAGGIE OPENED HER LAPTOP, LOGGED INTO HER banking Web site, and stared at the balance of her account, wishing the loan money wasn't dwindling so quickly. Tuition and books had eaten the majority of it. And last year's rent—for a dump of a place—had been much higher than she now paid Mrs. Norris. But here she stayed warm and dry. And safe. And fed.

Gooseflesh rose on her arms as all the hovels she'd called home paraded through her mind. Nothing like this house. This was by far the best. She'd hoped she could stay here until she finished writing her dissertation, sock away some cash to get a decent place after her hooding ceremony. But Mrs. Norris—Alicia—made it sound as if her time here would be shorter than anticipated.

Maybe she could pick up a few extra hours behind the bar at The Gingerbread Man during the holidays. Every dollar would count if she couldn't live here through the summer. But then, Alicia had only committed to her through May anyway. Maggie had only hoped for longer.

She shut her Internet browser and opened her project, due in three more days. Bare tree branches scraped the window in this bedroom-turned-office, and the wind howled in lament.

Maggie knew that sound. Or at least the feeling the sound inspired. It was the only part of being up north that she minded much. If she listened too long, it could send her to a dark place of longing.

She focused on other sounds, like the ones from downstairs, where the old woman moved from room to room decorating for a made-up holiday. Santa Claus had never done a thing for Maggie. Or the baby Jesus either. She saw no need to celebrate as if they had. But she could humor Alicia, seeing as she'd been good enough to open her home at such a reasonable rate.

Maggie moved her eyes back to the computer screen, concentrating on words and numbers.

At least until music wafted up from the bottom floor. A crooning singer waxing eloquently about old St. Nick. Maggie shook her head, her lips tightening in an attempt to concentrate. The song faded for a moment, and another swelled in its place. Maggie plugged her ears with her fingers as some woman sang about her "dear Savior's birth."

The droning continued for the next half hour. Maggie couldn't think. Finally, she snapped her laptop shut and shoved it into her messenger bag. Back to the library she would go.

"I'M SORRY. WAS THE MUSIC TOO LOU—" THE BACK door shut with a bang before Alicia could finish her apology. "Oh dear."

She plopped into the overstuffed chair nearest the fireplace. "Her" chair for so many years. She leaned into the worn fabric and propped her feet on the matching ottoman. She'd thought the music might cajole Maggie into a Christmas frame of mind, but the plan seemed to have gone awry.

"Sorry, Lord," she mumbled, then scrambled to her feet again. Best get as much accomplished as possible with the decorations before she ate the soup waiting in the slow cooker. She'd keep some back for Maggie too.

Almost two hours later, Alicia stacked the third empty tub atop the other two. Just a few more to go, but she needed a break.

At least she didn't have to stop and change the record, as they'd used to do. Not since Marcus had bought her an iPod and docking speakers and shown her how to use them. She ought to call and see how the kids' colds were and if Marcus had heard about the promotion at work yet. But she could do that later. Plenty of time.

In the kitchen, she lifted the glass lid from the warm crockpot and let the smell of tomatoes, veggies, and garlic fill the air. But when she opened the cabinet for a bowl, she remembered they were all in the dishwasher, still unwashed.

"Oh, bother." The extra bowls were higher up, away from arm's reach.

She grabbed the step stool from the laundry room and stood on the bottom rung. Still not high enough. She climbed up another step and reached for the edge of the stoneware bowl that sat on top of four others just like it.

Her fingers tipped the edge. The heavy bowls careened toward the countertop. Her body lurched backwards, away from the impending crash, disrupting her balance and sending her foot off the edge of the tread. Her arms windmilled, seeking balance but finding only air.

She crashed to the floor, pain shooting through her head, her back, her limbs. Flashes of light burst in front of her eyes.

Please, Lord. Help me. Help me.

She fought the pain, clinging to consciousness. *The button. I have to push the button.*

Her arm moved slowly, but it moved. She inched her fingers toward the string that circled her neck, the one attached to the device she'd railed against when Marcus and Daniel had insisted. But she had no strength to yank it free of her blouse. She felt for the plastic square and pushed as hard a she could through her heavy sweater.

Then her arm flopped back to the floor, her breath coming hard, spiraling with pain.

Someone would come. Someone would come soon.

MAGGIE SHOULDERED HER MESSENGER BAG AND trudged into the frigid night. Tiny snowflakes danced in the air around her. She pulled the frayed collar of her coat up around her ears, wishing she'd taken the time to wrap her scarf over her head. No matter. She just had get to the car as fast as possible.

Likely Alicia would have something hot waiting for her to eat. Her stomach rumbled at the thought. That woman could celebrate everything from National Peanut Butter Day to the Winter Solstice for all Maggie cared, as long as she let her live in that warm house with its soft bed and unending flow of hot water.

A high streetlight flooded the circle around her car with light, the rust streaks on the 1994 Sentra now tinted white.

And the front driver's side tire flat.

She wailed into the darkness before covering her face with mittened hands. When she raised her head to look again, the situation hadn't changed. See? No

Santa Claus. No Christ child. Just a mean world batter-ing her at every turn.

"Maggie? You okay?" a masculine voice called from across the parking lot.

She whirled to see Xavier Jones, her fellow teach-ing assistant, jogging toward her. When he reached her side, breath streamed white from his mouth and nose. She pointed in the direction of her car.

"That's not good," he said.

"No."

"You need a lift home?"

Frigid air knifed Maggie's lungs, reminding her how uncomfortable it would be to walk. Her shoulders slumped. "Yeah. If you don't mind."

He grinned, his ebony face in contrast to teeth the color of new snow. "You know I don't mind."

Yes, she knew. He'd asked her to dinner or coffee every day since they met in August. She'd turned him down every time. Until now.

But this wasn't a date, just a ride home. Him being in the right place in the right time.

"C'mon." He led the way to his vehicle, several years newer than hers but still not new. A grin twitched on her lips. The life of a grad student.

They drove in silence, Maggie thankful for a work-ing heater even for the short drive off campus.

As they turned the corner onto Evergreen Street, an ambulance pulled away from the curb in front of the house she called home.

"Wait!" Maggie fumbled with her seat belt and had the door half open before Xavier came to a complete stop. "Wait!" She ran after the flashing red and blue lights, but they soon outdistanced her.

She stopped in the middle of the street, hands cupping her knees. When she looked up again, the ambulance had disappeared. She glanced back at the house. Xavier stood in the front yard, her messenger bag hanging from his shoulder, while a woman bundled in a long puffy coat jabbered at him. Maggie squinted. The next-door neighbor. Maggie couldn't remember her name, but she'd know something.

Maggie joined them, trying to keep her panic leashed. "What happened?"

"She fell," the neighbor lady answered. "We found a step stool and broken bowls."

"Is she...is she...?" Maggie closed her eyes and swallowed.

Alicia had been kinder to her than almost anyone else in her life. Ever. She didn't want anything bad to happen to the old lady. Nor did she want to contemplate the mess her life would be if she had to move out now. During finals. With a miniscule bank balance. And a flat tire.

Merry Christmas to me.

"She came around for a minute when we all got there, but I don't know what kind of damage has been done."

Maggie nodded and swallowed hard. "Do I need to call anyone or do anything?"

The neighbor shook her head. "I have her sons' numbers. I'll let them know. I can keep you updated, if you want."

"That would be great."

The woman smiled and hurried back toward her house.

"Want me to come in with you?" Xavier asked. Maggie recognized his tone as friendly, nothing more, and that kindness threatened to undo her altogether.

She shook her head. "No, but thanks."

"Need a ride to campus tomorrow?" He walked backward, toward the street.

Instinct put a decline on the tip of her tongue, but she reeled it back. "I'd appreciate that."

"Nine o'clock sharp." He pointed at her over the top of his car.

Maggie raised a hand, then trudged inside.

The complete quiet of the house unnerved her, as did the shattered pieces of pottery scattered across the floor and counter. She'd best clean up a bit before scrounging some dinner. She found the broom and dustpan and cleared the biggest shards from the floor. As she dumped the pieces in the trash can, the phone on the wall trilled.

Maggie stared at it as her heart leaped into her throat. It rang again. And again.

She should answer it. She should. It might be one of Alicia's boys, though if they knew, why would they call here? One more ring, and the machine would pick up. Maybe she should let it.

But just before the click and whirr, she changed her mind, lifted the receiver. "Hello?"

"Oh, hello. Who is this?"

"Maggie. I'm Alic—Mrs. Norris's boarder."

"Oh yes, I remember now. This is Jenny, her daughter. Is Mom around?"

"Uh, no." Maggie's heart pumped faster. Jenny obviously hadn't heard about her mom's accident. But would she want to hear it from a stranger?

"Oh. Gone to the store, I guess? Or church. Doesn't matter. Tell her I just had her on my mind and—"

Maggie couldn't stand it any longer. "They just took your mama to the hospital."

"The hospital!"

"Yes. I don't know much. I got to the house as the ambulance pulled away."

"Ambulance?" Jenny's voice had shrunk now, sounding more like a child than a grown woman.

"She fell." Maggie's eyes roamed the kitchen. She spied the slow cooker in the cranny between the fridge and the corner, the contents bubbling merrily away. Her stomach rumbled even as her heart ached. Alicia had been carted away on a gurney, but a hot meal waited for Maggie. She didn't usually rate such good fortune. "The neighbor said she'd call your brothers."

"Yes. They'll know what to do. They'll call soon, I'm sure. I guess I should hang up, keep the line free."

"Probably best." Maggie suddenly wished she could do something more for Alicia, for her family.

"Thanks, Maggie. I'll—well, I can't do anything really. Except pray. Right?" Thin laughter, followed by what sounded like a gulped sob.

Maggie grunted what she hoped sounded like agreement before disconnecting. The family would pray. She, on the other hand, would slurp down a bowl of soup, finish cleaning the kitchen, and log more study time.

ALICIA COULDN'T REMEMBER WHEN SHE HAD LAST felt this young. No creak in her knees, no pain in her back, no stiffness in her wrists. She felt like laughing and twirling in the bright sunshine. So she did, the air just the right temperature, her long brown hair streaming around her.

From the corner of her eye, a man appeared. She stopped spinning.

"Fred!" She ran to him, young and lithe, and threw her arms around his sinewy neck. "Darling! I've missed you so much."

She couldn't remember where he'd been or why, but she didn't care.

She stroked his face and stared into his dark eyes. Then his lips brushed her cheek, only a whisper of a touch before he released himself from her arms. He took one step back. Then another, their fingertips slipping apart.

"No! Wait! I want to go with you!" Alicia's breath came faster, her heart pounding with fear that he'd leave her again. She ran to him and stopped only when his breath caressed her face.

The backs of his fingers trailed down her cheek. "You can't, dear. Not yet."

"But why? I don't understand." She wanted to cling to him, but her arms seemed glued to her sides, unable to obey the commands of her brain.

"You have a flower that needs some coaxing to bloom. It will be beautiful. You don't want to miss it."

His radiant smile warmed her and made her want something he deemed so good. But then she remembered the blanket of snow covering the yard.

"A flower? But the garden is dormant." She shook her head. "I can't even get to the soil until spring."

"Ah, but you already have, my darling. You already have."

He turned away and before she could protest, he had gone. The bright sunshine that canopied the field of green faded into white and gray and...noise.

Alicia turned her head, trying to quiet the incessant beeping. Her eyes opened to tubes and machines, a rail at the bedside, and the memory of a stack of bowls she couldn't quite reach.

THE MIDDLE OF THE NIGHT HAD NEVER BEEN MAGGIE'S friend. Not during her unsettled childhood or her turbulent teens or even the quiet of her college years, when she'd learned that to change her life she'd have to focus on the goal of education.

Fear lived in the middle of the night, along with doubt. They pummeled her desires, her dreams, told her she'd never reach that pinnacle of victory. They reminded her that while her name conjured up a bright-white, fragrant flower, her face more closely resembled the brown spot left on the petal by the touch of a human hand.

Magnolia. Why in the world had Mama chosen that name?

A fragile flower that needed a mild climate to survive. The name belonged to a girl with skin the color of milk and a heritage of privilege stretching back generations, not to one with a sordid family tree and a legacy of despair who lived in cold reality.

But she would rise above the past. A minority woman with a PhD, in engineering no less. She'd braved a man's domain on top of everything else. And her success would rocket her out of poverty and into security. Out of the fringe of society and into acceptance.

Acceptance by whom, she didn't have a clear picture. For once she reached that success, the few people who remained of her past would turn their backs on who she'd become. Either that or seek to profit from her climb out of the pit.

Maggie stared at the ceiling over her bed, arms folded behind her head. No one had called to update her on Alicia. Did that mean she still breathed? Knowing Alicia, the old lady was sitting up in bed laughing at herself.

Maggie rolled over, fighting thoughts of tests and projects, of flat tires and precarious living situations. Even fighting thoughts of Xavier's dark eyes.

She threw off the covers and her feet found the worn slippers next to the bed. She shrugged into a cheap terry cloth robe and cinched it tight. If sleep wouldn't come, she'd do something useful. Something for Alicia. For her constant kindness and generosity.

Tiptoeing down the stairs, Maggie suddenly remembered she needn't be quiet. No one would hear. So she tromped across the floor toward the kitchen, stopping at the living room. She clicked the lamp on low.

A Santa Claus figurine, complete with a bulging pack on his back, sat nearby. A three-foot Christmas tree rose from a round table draped with a green cloth. A trio of angels on an evergreen garland hung over the mantel. Two boxes cluttered the middle of the room, their tops discarded, tissue paper draped over the sides and scattered on the floor.

Maggie stepped closer and peered into the boxes. Cardboard dividers filled with ornaments. An elaborate angel probably meant for the tree's top sat on a nearby table. She lifted a snowflake from the box, three Popsicle sticks glued together, painted blue, and sprinkled with glitter. She turned it over in her hand. *Jenny, 1976* was scrawled on the back. She held the gold ribbon loop and let the child's craft dangle from her fingers. It twisted and twirled, the glitter catching the lamplight.

Maggie looked up at the bare branches of the artificial tree and knew what she could do. Even if Alicia didn't live, her children would appreciate coming home to one last Christmas that looked familiar. One last gift from a mother who loved them the way Maggie always dreamt of being loved.

The box emptied. The tree filled. Maggie sat back and studied her work. Sufficient, she imagined. At least she'd done something, and that sparked a bit of the peace that so often eluded her grasp.

After two trips, all the empty tubs had been relegated to the basement. When she returned to the living room, a wide yawn reminded her of her early morning. Still time to catch a quick nap.

But as she surveyed the room one last time she noticed the dark figurines parading across the mantel—and the white envelope set in their midst.

Curiosity drew her toward the display. She knew enough to realize this was the stable scene, the "Happy birthday, Jesus" moment. But the set didn't look anything like others she'd seen. She couldn't keep her fingers from the crudely carved faces of the people, the unusual shape of the animals, the hut-like enclosure.

Then her gaze moved to the envelope. *For Mom*, it read, loopy letters in stark contrast to the snowy paper. A girl's handwriting. From Jenny, maybe?

Snatching the envelope, Maggie carried it to the sofa and sat. She turned it over in her hands before tugging the enclosed page free.

No date at the top. But on the back, *Love, Jenny,* just as she'd suspected.

> *Dear Mom,*
>
> *I hope you like this nativity set I picked up on my trip to Ghana. It is mahogany, carved by a local artist. Different from what you are used to, I know, but quite beautiful in its own right. Or at least I thought so. But they are more than just another reminder of why we celebrate Jesus' birth, Mom. They are the reason I have to go back.*

Maggie leaned back, her breath catching in her throat. Had Alicia done the same as she read the words? Her only daughter, living a world away. Alicia had been proud to tell Maggie of Jenny's work with young girls in desperate circumstances, but she'd also sensed that Alicia missed her daughter. Probably more since her husband had passed away.

> *When I stood in the market that day, I'd had no other thought than bringing you a present from my trip. A good trip, but to that point, not necessarily a life-changing one. I saw this and knew you'd be pleased. But as the gentleman told his story of selling his carvings so that*

he and his wife could care for girls with no other means of support—girls destined for prostitution—my heart squeezed and tears filled my eyes. And I knew. I could help with my degrees in social work and psychology and my heart for evangelism. You told me God would use my gifts for something special. We just never dreamed it would be something special on the other side of the world.

I love you, Mom, and I know I don't need your permission to go, but I want your blessing. Yours and Dad's. I need to know you are both behind me, praying for me, loving me. That's all I want for Christmas, from now and forevermore.

Love, Jenny

Maggie stared at the page. Obviously Alicia and her husband had sent Jenny off with their blessing. Her gaze returned to the manger scene above the fireplace. She knew Alicia went to church and bought into all that religion stuff, though she'd never shoved it in Maggie's face or made her feel guilty. She'd accepted Maggie's life with the same apparent graciousness she did her daughter's decision to move to Africa and save trafficked girls. Maggie bit her lip, considering.

Baby Jesus had never done anything to help Maggie, but if He could help Alicia, wouldn't that be the same thing?

She rose. With a deep breath, she lifted the small figurine carved into a rectangular bed of straw and let it rest in the palm of her hand, praying the first prayer of her pitiful life.

"I'M SO SORRY, MARCUS. I HATE THAT I PULLED YOU away from work at such a busy time of year." Alicia leaned on her eldest son's arm as he led her from the car to her house after three days in the hospital.

He patted her arm and kissed her cheek. "I'm just glad you weren't seriously injured." He glanced up at the big stone house. "But are you sure you should be back here alone?"

"I'm not alone. I told you, my boarder, Maggie, will be here all through the holidays. By the time she's busy with classes again, my ribs will be fully healed."

He crooked an eyebrow at her. "She won't be working? I always had to work breaks during grad school."

"I hadn't thought about that. You're probably right." Alicia sighed, feeling as if she'd lived much longer than three-quarters of a century. Then a plan lit her mind like fireworks in a dark sky. She smiled at Marcus, feeling lighter, younger. "If she needs to work, I'll pay her to babysit me instead."

The idea warmed Alicia more thoroughly than the thought of days in her easy chair near the roaring fire and a stack of books beside her. Yes, time with Maggie would be the perfect occupation. Time to warm the girl's heart the way the spring sunshine would eventually soften the ground, ready it for seed.

Marcus stopped at the bottom of the three steps leading to the kitchen door. "If you're sure. You know Cindy and I would be happy to have you at our house while you recuperate. Daniel and Lily said the same."

"No, I'll get better rest here, in my own bed. In the quiet." Alicia's gaze roamed the exterior of her home until it blurred beneath unshed tears. "I know I can't stay here forever, but I need time to say good-bye. At least give me that."

Marcus nodded and held her elbow as she lifted her feet, grimacing with each step. At least she hadn't broken her hip like her friend Marielle had last year. Marielle hadn't yet been released from the rehab center.

Alicia stepped over the threshold, expecting a quiet chill in the almost uninhabited house. Maggie would have spent much of the past few days at the library, though Marcus had called and told her they would arrive home this morning.

Instead, the smell of fresh-baked cookies greeted her nose, and the crackle and pop of a fire reached her ears. She looked at Marcus. "Did you come here first?"

He shook his head, shut the door, then slid Alicia's coat from her arms. She stood in the middle of the kitchen, seeing no sign at all of the mess she'd left behind.

"Bed or chair?" Marcus asked.

"Chair, definitely. Three days in bed was quite enough, thank you." Alicia shuffled toward the living room, the blaze in the fireplace drawing her with its cheery welcome. When she entered the room fully, her feet refused to move further.

Her tree sparkled in the corner, all the old, sentimental ornaments dangling from the branches. No empty boxes waited to be carried downstairs. And Bing Crosby crooned quietly from the speakers on the bookshelf, wishing her a white Christmas.

Alicia gripped Marcus's arm more tightly. "Who—who did this?"

"I did," came the quiet answer from behind them. Arms folded over her chest, Maggie leaned her shoulder into the door frame, her bottom lip caught between her teeth.

"Oh, Maggie. It's . . . it's . . ."

Marcus smiled at Maggie, then urged Alicia to her chair, helped her settle in before draping a velour throw over her legs.

Maggie took another step into the room. "I didn't know exactly how you liked things, but I tried."

Alicia held out her hand in invitation. "You did it beautifully. Such a wonderful surprise. A wonderful gift." She squeezed Maggie's fingers.

Maggie's chin dropped to her chest. Was she embarrassed? Pleased?

Marcus cleared his throat. "Maggie, right?" He stuck out his hand. "Short for Margaret?"

Her head shot up, black curls dancing around her delicate face. Wariness colored her eyes as a blush stole up her neck and into her cheeks. "Um, Magnolia, actually."

Magnolia. That delicate Southern flower.

Alicia's chest tightened. Magnolia. Maggie. Her flower.

Alicia held her breath, praying Maggie would hear Marcus out—and that she'd accept the task.

"As you can see, my mother needs someone to care for her until she is back to full speed. She suggested you."

Maggie's gaze found Alicia's.

"Of course, I'll pay you." Alicia straightened the blanket draped over her legs. "I'd be your job for the winter break—unless you'd rather do something else."

Maggie's almond-shaped eyes rounded. "You'd—*pay* me just to live here?"

"Yes, to help Mom. Do some light housekeeping and cooking, of course." Marcus's phone beeped. He excused himself from the room.

The flame hissed for a moment, then returned to the normal crackle.

"I need you, Maggie," Alicia said. "Will you help me?"

Alicia's heart pinched as she followed Maggie's gaze to the top of the mantel, to Jenny's nativity set and the letter set among the figurines. Maggie stepped toward the mantel and fingered the tiny baby Jesus. A shudder shook the young woman's delicate frame, followed by a deep breath.

When Maggie raised her head, she smiled. A real smile. A radiant smile. The bud of a beautiful flower Alicia prayed would soon find full bloom.

PROMISES, PROMISES
Liz Johnson

George Meade had made Susanna Harkins three promises when he asked her to marry him on Christmas Eve thirty-two years ago. He vowed he would love her forever, make every Christmas special, and teach her to ride a motorcycle.

In that snow-covered gazebo on the town's public square, he'd immediately begun fulfilling those promises. The delight of Christmas was magnified by the joy of their engagement, sharing with both friends and family that first year. The next thirty were filled with kids and jobs, joy and the business of life. And while the third promise had fallen to the wayside as they raised two little ones, she'd never had cause to doubt that he would keep his word.

Until this year.

Susanna flicked back the curtain over the front window and peered down the dark street. Again. Still no headlights. Still no motion. Only multicolored, dancing lights reflected off waist-high snowdrifts that lined the residential lane. The neighboring homes were only half as festive as usual with so many lawn decorations covered by the relentless white.

And while George had always strung icicle lights across the eaves of their ranch home and placed a spotlight on a wooden manger scene in the lawn, this year the Meade home boasted only an evergreen wreath with a red bow on the front door. A poor showing of Christmas spirit, if anyone asked Susie.

Which they hadn't.

She sighed, letting the curtain fall back into place as she wandered back to the couch and plopped down in front of her favorite Christmas movie. It seemed a guarantee that *White Christmas* could be found on at least one television channel every hour of every day during the winter holidays. Bing Crosby and Danny Kaye danced and sang their way around a Vermont resort, while Susie checked her phone for a new message.

Only the one quick line from George.

Running late. Still at work. Be home as soon as I can.

He was probably held up by another wife, who had decided to buy her husband a riding mower or something like it for Christmas. As the number-one small-tractor salesman in the entire state of Iowa, George put in long hours. He'd never missed decorating the tree before, though.

With or without him, she couldn't put off the night's tasks any longer. Ambling down the hall, she opened the linen closet, then dragged two giant plastic tubs toward the living room. They left distinct tracks in the carpet as she stumbled and wrestled to get them into place in front of the seven-foot spruce, which remained bare just ten days before the biggest holiday of the year.

With the lids popped off, the bins displayed a wealth of memories. Everything from Gabriel's kindergarten handprint to Anita's glittering orange angel had been rigged up on fishing line and lovingly hung from pine branches year after year. Thirty-two years of memories—thirty-one perfect Christmases—wasn't a bad run.

Except she wanted more.

George had promised more. He'd promised *always*.

As she hooked a miniature green-and-yellow tractor on a sturdy branch, the kitchen door swung open, a blast of cold air speared through her, and she hunched her shoulders against the chill.

"Sorry I'm late, hon." George let his boots fall to the floor with matching thuds as he hung his down coat on the hook in the mudroom. "Did you start without me?"

Susie grumbled something under her breath so low that even she didn't know exactly what she was saying. But the sentiment was clear.

He ran past the covered dinner plate on the stove and through the living room to plant a kiss on the top of her head. His hand on her cheek as warm and gentle as it had been all those years ago, he looked straight into her eyes and smiled. "I'm sorry that I missed decorating the Christmas tree with you. I hurried home as fast as I could." His gaze swung over the memory-laden branches. "Looks good."

She shrugged, but didn't pull away from his touch as he slipped his arm around her waist. "There are still a few left to put up."

He bent and scooped up a hand-crafted ornament, holding it out as if to ask where it should go. His callused hand dwarfed the walnut shell, which served as a makeshift manger for a tiny baby doll swaddled in a miniature blanket. "Anita made this, didn't she?"

"I think she was five." Susie pointed to an open spot near the star.

"Oh yes." He winked as he caught the yarn loop between sharp needles. "That was a good Christmas."

A tiny smile forced its way through her scowl. "That was twenty-three years ago. How do you remember?"

George's green eyes sparkled with mischief. "They've all been good with you."

But would they continue that way? Only time would tell, but she didn't know if her Christmas spirit could hold on long enough to find out.

When the last figurine was in place, George closed up the storage tubs with a broad smile. His beard had a little more gray than it used to, but the joy of the season seemed to fill every wrinkle, new and old.

"What kept you late tonight?"

His smile flickered, something like excitement flashing through his eyes. "It's a busy time of year. Lots to be done."

"Do you think it'll stay so busy? Will you be able to help me deliver cookies to the neighbors Thursday night?"

He gave her a peck on the cheek before carrying the empty bins back to their storage spot. "I'll do my best."

GEORGE'S BEST TURNED INTO APOLOGETIC PHONE calls and yet another night he would be delayed coming home. Susie stared through the same foggy window, down the same empty street. The scent of fresh pumpkin bread mingled with the sharply sweet fragrance of frosted sugar cookies and filled the empty house.

It looked like George would be just as late as he had been the night before. And the two before that. That left Susie with two options. She could either eat her way through the perfectly arranged treat trays or deliver them herself.

With a sigh, she shrugged into her warmest coat, wrapped a scarf around her neck, and slipped on her snow boots. Her college days as a waitress served her well as she balanced six trays on one arm and navigated her way through the side door and along the slippery walkway. Fat snowflakes dropped from a gray sky, sticking to her scarf and coating the plastic-wrapped cookies.

Past air-filled snowmen, white-light reindeer, and even a dancing penguin, she visited every door in the cul-de-sac, wishing each family a merry Christmas and a very happy New Year until there was only one plate left. One bell left to ring.

Mary Beth Tremble.

The old woman never failed to offer up a litany of complaints and woes. No matter how much Susie didn't want to hear about Gloria's son's money troubles or how Frank's granddaughter had been left at the altar, Mary Beth always insisted on sharing. George had perfected the art of keeping the conversation to harmless topics and uplifting news. But he wasn't there.

Standing in front of Mary Beth's undecorated house—her only holiday concession a green lightbulb illuminating her porch—Susie glanced toward the far street corner. Her pulse thrummed as she waited for a pair of truck headlights to turn onto their street. *Please, let George get here soon.*

But he didn't.

And the cold began to seep through her coat, setting her teeth to chattering and her skin tingling.

Trudging up the steps, she steeled herself for the interaction with her neighbor, practicing her brief holiday wishes. She pressed the pad of her finger to the doorbell, and the chime sang like an overzealous red-kettle bell ringer.

"Coming. On my way." Mary Beth's voice called out from deep in the otherwise silent house.

"Be right there."

Something twisted around Susie's heart at the urgency in the older woman's voice. Susie was a new empty nester with a mysteriously absent husband. But Mary Beth had been widowed years before, and in all the years she'd lived next door, Mary Beth had rarely received visitors.

Susie pushed a genuine smile into place as Mary Beth opened the door. "Merry Christmas!" She held out the cookies.

"Oh, you're such a dear. Thank you." Mary Beth pressed her nose to the plastic wrap as though she could inhale the sweets. "Come in out of the cold and have a cup of tea with me."

Susie opened her mouth to decline, but the twinge in her chest snapped it closed. It was a sad day when she couldn't afford fifteen minutes for a lonely woman. "All right. Just a quick one."

"Wonderful." Mary Beth's tottering steps led the way into the dim house that smelled of equal parts mothballs and cinnamon. "Sit down."

Susie eyed the plastic-covered sofa before settling onto the edge of a recliner in the living room. "Can I help with something?"

"Not at all. I already had water boiling." Mary Beth disappeared into the kitchen, but her voice never stopped. "I haven't seen you around lately. You've probably been busy wrapping up the semester at school."

"My second-graders sure keep me busy, and I think we're all thankful for the winter break."

Mary Beth reappeared, carrying a tray with two mugs and several of the cookies Susie had decorated that morning. "And George?"

"Oh, he's..." Her voice trailed off. Busy? Delayed? Absent? All fit, and all made the band around her heart tighten.

Apparently Mary Beth wasn't overly interested in the response to her question, as she handed Susie a steaming mug and barreled on. "Fred Majors said he saw George at the bowling alley Monday night."

Sweet peppermint tea singed her tongue, and Susie sputtered into her cup. "The bowling alley?"

One cosmetically enhanced eyebrow—penciled in black, and out of place below a head of white curls—rose, wrinkling Mary Beth's forehead even more than normal. "In the parking lot."

Swallowing the lump in her throat, Susie put on a good show, plastering a smile into place and nodding quickly behind her cup. "Of course. The bowling alley. Yes. On Monday. How is Fred?"

Mary Beth squinted as though she wasn't entirely convinced, but after a short pause, she plunged into the news of Fred's most recent medical crisis. For her part, Susie heard none of it. The mug in her hands had turned instantly cold, and all the air in the room seemed to have vanished.

What was George doing at the bowling alley when he'd told her he was working late? He'd missed decorating the tree for *bowling*?

The questions rang over and over in her mind, consuming her. She would have no peace until she knew exactly what was going on with her husband.

THE NEXT MORNING, WHEN SUSIE ASKED GEORGE what was keeping him late at work every night so close to Christmas, he slid his arm around her shoulder and kissed her nose. "You know how it is this time of year," he said before slipping out the side door and leaving for work.

As she pushed her shopping cart through the grocery store later that day, picking up the pasta and sauce for their traditional Italian Christmas Eve dinner, the stone in her stomach began to grow. Up and down every aisle, all she saw was George's lie. Every blind corner just emphasized the truth he hid from her.

Thirty-two years, and this was how he kept his promises? This was how he thought he'd make Christmas special? If he thought he could get away with ruining her holidays, he had another think coming.

As she tossed a package of chicken breasts into her cart, she tried to come up with a plan for catching George. He'd been particularly tight-lipped lately, so she was going to have to do more than ask.

Suddenly a little boy pushing a miniature cart barreled around an end cap. He looked over his shoulder, never slowing down. An instant later, a frazzled young mom raced after him, hot on his trail.

As an idea began to take shape, Susie's feet picked up speed. She could follow him. Keep a tail on him until she figured out what he was doing and put an end to this farce of a Christmas celebration. One way or another.

With the decision made, she practically ran through the checkout line before racing to her car, nearly overturning a red kettle on the way. Mumbling an apology to the flabbergasted bell ringer, she kept plowing forward. Her old sedan rattled and groaned as she floored it the two miles home to drop off her groceries in the kitchen. Then she headed back out into the cold. George's shift was scheduled to end shortly, and if he left the office before she got there, she'd never be able to find him.

George's tractor dealership sat on the far side of town, where the neighborhoods began to thin, replaced by straight rows of corn and soybeans in the summer. In the winter a thick layer of white covered the fields while farmers prayed for a warm spring and enough summer rain for a rich harvest.

Susie drove past the sales office, slowing down to check for George's red truck, which was still parked in his normal spot, as far from the office entrance as possible. Always courteous to the customers, saving them a few frigid steps.

A frown tugged at her mouth, and she heaved a sigh as she pulled off the rural road, parking where she would just be able to see when he left. Why did it seem he was more interested in being kind to customers than to his own wife?

Minutes ticked by like hours, and the sky opened up, pouring a blanket of snow upon her car until her windshield wipers could barely keep her line of sight clear. Maybe she should just go home. Visibility dwindled, and she'd never be able to keep her eye on him anyway.

Just then a flash of red caught her attention.

George's truck lumbered down the gravel drive before pulling onto the crossroad and heading toward home.

She wasn't going to get a better invitation than this.

Pulling out behind him, she kept just enough distance between them to maintain sight of his truck. George didn't make any indication that he realized she was there, so she kept up the tail down Main Street and then into an industrial section of town. Mechanic shops and short grain silos peppered the roads, and when George pulled off to park in front of a small metal barn, Susie had to drive past or risk being discovered. Just as she found a place to turn around, her phone rang.

The tiny screen flashed with George's picture, and she put her car in park as she answered it. "Hello?"

"Hi, sweetheart. How was your day?"

"My day? Oh, um, fine."

He paused. Did she sound strange? Could he tell that she was less than a block away? Finally he continued. "Do you need me to run by the store on my way home to pick up anything else for Christmas Eve?"

"No. I shopped earlier today. Are you on your way home now?" A loud clank rang through her phone, and she jumped. "What was that?"

"Er...nothing."

Right. *Nothing.* She'd believe that when Iowa saw a Christmas that was sunny and seventy-five degrees.

After another jarring thump, he said, "I have to go. There's lots left to do tonight. But I'll be home as soon as I can. Shouldn't be more than an hour."

Susie hung up the phone and waited for any sign of George's truck rolling back out the short drive, but it didn't reappear. Snowdrifts seemed to grow exponentially, but there was no sign of the cherry-red four-by-four. With each tick of her watch, the cold seeped further and further into her car until her fingers grew numb and her nose lost all feeling.

This was a lost cause. She wasn't going to discover George's secret today. It was better to throw in the towel than end up snowed in on the side of an almost deserted road.

As she rolled past the lot where George had parked twenty minutes earlier, she spotted the name on the small building, emblazoned in green paint over a white garage door: Bunting Snow Removal and Landscaping.

She'd never heard of them, and she paid all of the bills every month.

Was he wrapped up in something that he couldn't tell her about? Or had he just forgotten that he'd promised to make Christmas special every year? And if he'd forgotten that, had he forgotten his other promises too?

Suddenly George appeared, strolling from the office door toward a big white truck, which had been fitted with a snowplow on its front bumper. She nearly swallowed her tongue. What on earth was he doing?

He started the monstrous vehicle and backed it out of its parking spot as though he had every right to sit behind the wheel. Susie ducked her head, hoping he wouldn't recognize her as the truck pulled out onto the road behind her.

She kept her speed up, trying not to let him get close enough to read her license plate between the snowflakes, but he tailed her like a pro. Her heart thudded heavy in her chest and her hands began sweating as if she'd been found out.

Only she wasn't the one with anything to hide.

He followed her until she was certain he had iden-
tified her car, and just as she steeled herself to explain
why *she* had followed *him*, the white truck in her rearview turned into the snow-covered parking lot of a
small strip mall. Stopped at a light, she watched him
lower the plow and set to work clearing the deserted
spaces.

The truth dawned on her like the morning sun
fighting through fog, slow and strange.

George had a second job. One he hadn't told her
about.

UNSURE HOW TO BROACH THE SUBJECT WITH HER
husband, Susie spent three days hinting around at his
extracurricular activities, only to be brushed aside
with a grin and chuckle. He assured her all was well
and he was just at work.

It wasn't exactly a lie. He was working. At least, she
assumed he was being paid for plowing parking lots.

But it most certainly wasn't the whole truth, and
Susie didn't know how to deal with anything less. Like
a fall leaf blown about by the wind, she followed every
little clue and minor lead until she found one worthy
of pouncing on.

The lead that finally stuck was a message from
the sales assistant at the dealership. On the morning

before Christmas Eve day, Susie missed the phone when it rang, but after the machine's beep, Jenna's voice rang loud and clear throughout the house. "George, it's Jenna. Craig called. He needs to meet you at a pub instead of his shop. It's on the corner of Sixth Avenue and Woodlawn. I'll call your cell in case you've already left."

Craig, huh? He sounded like someone up to no good.

Grabbing her binoculars and an extra scarf in case she had to sit in her car for a while, Susie headed for the location of the pub Jenna indicated. Susie wasn't sure what time their meeting was, but as long as George hadn't traded out his truck for another vehicle, she would be able to find him.

Of course, nothing was a given any longer.

As she pulled into a parking spot across the street from Bubba's Grub and Grill, Susie had no trouble spotting her husband. He was the one who looked entirely out of place in the lot of a run-down two-story building. The railing on the second-story balcony sagged in the middle, while neon flashing signs in the windows boasted favorite beverages on tap. It was the only building on the block that offered no hint of Christmas cheer, and the patrons seemed to know the dress code involved leather.

George, in his crisp gray suit and bright-red tie, fit in as well as a minnow in a shark tank. But his strides were firm as he walked over to shake hands with a large man in a jean vest and plaid flannel shirt. He thumped George on the back, and the men seemed to laugh at the greeting.

Susie pressed her binoculars to her face, focusing in on their expressions. Both men wore neutral grins, and George moved toward his truck. Craig followed him, and they both bent over to stare at the bumper.

Which, even through the binoculars, looked like any ordinary bumper.

She'd give anything to hear their conversation, but her private-eye skills lacked any real professionalism, so she was stuck trying to read their lips.

Craig repeated the same mouth motion several times, and it looked like he was talking about a guy named Mike. He gestured broadly toward the big wooden door of Bubba's.

Maybe Mike was inside.

George shook his head and hiked his thumb over his shoulder.

Apparently he didn't want to meet Mike. And shouldn't he be at work, anyway?

The wind picked up the snow at their feet, sending flurries around their shins, and Craig crossed his massive arms, stretching the plaid of his shirt for all it was worth.

While Craig continued talking, George pulled a thick white envelope out of his jacket's front pocket, and Susie's stomach lurched. He passed it to Craig, who opened it and went through the universal motions of counting the contents. There was money in there. Quite possibly the money that George had been making on his side job. The job he hadn't told her about.

As the men parted ways, her mind jumped to the very worst possibility.

George was being blackmailed.

"Oh, don't be silly." The words and following chuckle echoed in her otherwise silent car. Rural Iowa didn't have blackmailers. And if it did, they wouldn't be foolish enough to meet on the corner of a busy street, in front of a pub doing a good lunch business. And George wouldn't have shaken hands and had a conversation with a man trying to swindle him.

Craig clapped George on the shoulder as they parted ways, as if to display the ridiculousness of her notion.

So if it wasn't blackmail, then what had George out of the office during one of the busiest sales seasons, giving money to a stranger?

If she didn't find out soon, she was going to burst. And her loving husband was likely to be on the receiving end of that explosion.

ON CHRISTMAS EVE MORNING, SUSIE FINISHED wrapping up the presents she'd bought for George. A Swiss army knife that he'd been eyeing at the hunting store for several months. A beautiful leather wallet to replace the one he'd been using since before Gabe was born. The military history book by the author they'd seen interviewed on television the month before. George had talked about the interview for days.

They were small gifts, but she didn't doubt that he'd appreciate them. At least the old George would appreciate them.

When the last gift was wrapped and the final bow tied into place, Susie tucked the festive boxes under the tree. She glanced around to make sure that George was still down the hall in their bedroom before sneaking a peek at the tags on the other packages below the lowest branches. Scooting around to the boxes that had appeared days before, she flipped up the tags.

To Mom. Love, Anita and Joe.

To Mom and Dad. We love you! Gabe and family.

On they went. And not a single one for her from George.

Her shoulders sagged, and she fought tears that threatened to spill down her cheeks. It wasn't about the gifts or the lack thereof. It wasn't about the money spent or even the time he put into it.

As she hugged her knees to her chest, she squeezed her eyes shut against the pain that boiled within. She didn't need his gifts. All she really wanted for Christmas was a reminder that he hadn't forgotten his promises.

George's footfalls in the hallway caught her attention, and she quickly swiped under her eyes and ran her fingers through her hair.

"Good morning, sunshine." He walked across the living room and bent to press a kiss to the top of her head. "Merry Christmas Eve."

"Merry Christmas Eve to you too." She tried to get her smile to stay in place, but it wiggled and squirmed like it refused to be part of a lie. "What are we going to do today?" It felt like a lifetime since he'd had a real day off, and she couldn't suppress the flicker of hope that welled inside at the prospect of spending an entire day with the man she loved.

He plopped down on the couch next to her and tapped his chin. "Well, I have to run an errand this afternoon, and then I thought we could go to the later Christmas Eve service."

Her hope burst and any façade of a smile vanished. Susie crossed her arms over her chest and shook her head. "What errand?"

He winked at her, his grin just like Gabe's had been when he'd snuck a cookie from the jar. "I'll tell you about it later."

"Well, why don't I go with you?" She hated the pleading tone of her voice, and cleared her throat to try to get it under control. "Then at least we'll get to spend the day together."

George's eyebrows pinched together, as if he were in deep thought. But his answer came quickly and definitively. "I'm sorry. This is one of those things I have to do on my own."

"Like everything else you've been doing the last few weeks?" The words shot out before she even knew they were on the tip of her tongue, and her pleading had been replaced by the bitterness she'd been pushing down and an anger that refused to be ignored. "Like hanging out at the bowling alley when you promised to help me decorate the tree? Like driving a truck that isn't yours? Or meeting with strange men in the middle of the day?"

His mouth dropped open, and a hoarse laugh escaped. "How do you know about all of that?"

"I followed you."

His laugh turned true and full, until his eyes nearly disappeared beneath the humor that covered his face. "Of course you did. And I love you for it." He reached for her hand, but she pulled hers away, hopping to her feet.

"I want to know what's going on, and I want to know why you decided this was the year you'd ruin Christmas."

"Then come with me on my errand."

"Well, now I don't want to." If it was a woman's prerogative to change her mind, Susie would take full advantage of it. At the moment she wanted to be about as far away from George as she could get. Marching toward the kitchen, she picked up her purse and pulled on her coat.

"Where are you going?" he asked.

"Anywhere but here." She flew out the front door, slamming it behind her and rattling the entire house before running down the steps, getting into her car, and racing down the street.

She didn't have a clue where she was going, tears streaming down her cheeks. They hadn't had a fight like that in years. Maybe she'd been too sensitive and let her emotions run away with her. But he had to know that he'd hurt her.

If this George—the one who neglected Christmas and his wife—was the new norm, her whole life would change. And she didn't want it to. She loved her husband and her life just the way they were. Sure, they'd changed over the years, but George had always been stable and dependable. And he'd always lived up to his word.

Her car seemed to find its own way to the middle of town and the vast park in front of the courthouse. The gazebo on the lawn twinkled with white lights, and buckets of poinsettias covered the front steps. Not much had changed since George had proposed to her in that very spot thirty-two years before.

Susie parked her car and slipped from behind the wheel, strolling toward the wooden structure. She was already to the bottom step when she saw another young couple sitting on the bench along the east wall. They were so young, barely adults, yet so familiar.

Suddenly the young man dipped to his knee and held out a ring. "Would you marry me, Rosie?"

The girl squealed the glee of every woman in love and threw her arms around his neck. "Of course, I will. Yes!"

Susie sidestepped her destination and the memories it held, instead circling the base of the elevated gazebo as the wind nipped at her cheeks and cooled the heat of her anger. As she walked, she whispered a prayer for the two to hold tight to the promises they were about to make.

Because both made promises—just as she and George had. He wasn't the only one to make a vow on a long ago Christmas Eve. She'd promised to love him too.

Even when she didn't understand him.

By the time she arrived home, George was gone, almost certainly off on his mysterious errand. And the kitchen called. She fought the urge to forgo the grand Italian meal in favor of a simple cup of soup. Instead, she pulled out the meat and breading ingredients to make chicken parmesan. George's favorite. Mozzarella and tomato sauce bubbled and mingled, the rich aroma of Italian herbs wrapping her up like a cocoon. The warmth of the oven, like a blanket, soothed her aching heart and reminded her of the years she'd spent in this same kitchen with her two best helpers.

She could almost see Anita's tiny hands measuring out the cheese. And Gabe's fists pounding graham crackers into the perfect cheesecake crust.

Whether he was home or not, George had given her the two best miracles of her life. And as she set the two places at the table for their first Christmas Eve alone, she smiled. This is what Christmas was all about—loving someone first, whether he deserved it or not.

Just as she pulled the chicken from the oven and poured the dressing on the Caesar salad, the roar of George's truck echoed around the cul-de-sac. Perfect timing.

He swung the front door open, then slammed it against the burst of cold that whipped into the house, which seemed to groan under the weight of weeks of snow. "You're back!" he announced. "Good. I have something to show you."

Her forehead wrinkled, and she frowned. "Dinner's ready. Let's eat and then you can show me."

"I've been waiting weeks for this." His tone turned cajoling, but she didn't budge from her spot at the counter.

"Then another hour won't matter." She carried the salad to the table and filled each of their glasses.

"It will. Come with me. It'll only take a minute."

"But the food will get cold." He wiggled his eyebrows, and she couldn't help but laugh. "Fine."

He held out her jacket, helping her into each arm before kneeling to slide her feet from her slippers into her snow boots. Then he led her outside. She turned to pull the door closed, giving it an extra hard tug—and spun as the whole world crashed down around them.

She caught only a glimpse of two shining chrome motorcycles on a trailer attached to the back of George's truck before the wall of snow that had piled up on top of the garage gave a painful groan and plummeted to the driveway. She shrieked and latched on to George's arm as his eyes grew wide. When the avalanche settled, his big surprise was wheel-deep in snow, but two beautiful bodies and matching sets of handlebars still glowed in the bright light over the garage.

She couldn't keep a giggle from escaping. "Oops." She threw her hand over her mouth. "I think I've been loosening that with all my door slamming this week."

His features slowly transformed from shock to humor. Pulling her into his arms, he serenaded her with great belly laughs. "Oh, my sweet Susanna."

"Is this what you've been doing? All this time?"

He nodded. "When I found these, I knew they were perfect. But they were a little more than I had saved up, so I took some extra work plowing parking lots at the bowling alley and a couple strip malls."

"Oh, George, I've been so bitter, thinking you just didn't care about me or Christmas, thinking you forgot your promises. But you've been working all along—to make Christmas special."

He kissed the tip of her nose. "Always."

"You didn't forget."

"Never."

That night as they dug their matching motorcycles out of the snowbank and cleaned and dried them, George looked up at Susie and caught her gaze. His smile was warm and tender, and it renewed every promise he'd made. *I will always love you. I will make every Christmas we share special. And I will teach you to ride this motorcycle. Starting right now.*

She'd thought she was showing him love when he didn't deserve it, but really, he had loved her when *she* didn't deserve it. Like another Father had on a Christmas two thousand years before, George had kept his promise. Maybe that's what love—what Christmas—was all about.

About the Authors

Susan Call ("Secondhand Miracle") is the author of *A Search for Purple Cows, A True Story of Hope* (Guidepost Books, 2013). An inspirational speaker, Susan is also a hobby photographer. She holds a Master of Science in Marriage and Family Therapy. Originally from Pennsylvania, she now calls New Hampshire home.

Ashley Clark ("Christmas Dreams") writes stories with Southern grace. When she's not writing, Ashley enjoys teaching literature courses at her local university, rescuing stray animals, and finding charming new towns. She lives on the Gulf Coast with her husband, Matthew, and two rescued dogs, Maddie and Schroeder. Learn more about Ashley at ashleyclarkfiction.com.

Anita Mae Draper ("Here We Come A-Wassailing") lives on the Canadian prairies where she writes both historical and contemporary stories inspired by the Western landscape and family genealogy. Anita is honored to have a second story chosen for A Cup of Christmas Cheer series. You can find Anita at anitamaedraper.com.

Sarah Forgrave ("Ring of Kindness") is a work-at-home mom who feels blessed to do what she loves—raise her two children while writing stories that inspire. Her credits include contributions to the webzine *Ungrind* and the Pearl Girls book *Mother of Pearl: Luminous Lessons and Iridescent Faith*. When not writing, she enjoys teaching fitness classes and spending time with her family in their Midwest home.

Carla Olson Gade ("The Memory Shop") is the author of two novels and two novellas, including the best-selling *Mistletoe Memories*. She also contributed to Guidepost Books' *A Cup of Christmas Cheer: Tales of Faith and Family for the Holidays* ("Upon a Christmas Tree Schooner"). A native New Englander, she writes from her home in rural Maine and enjoys historical research, genealogy, and photography. You may connect with Carla at carlagade.com.

Liz Johnson ("Promises, Promises") is the author of seven novels and a handful of short stories. An

Arizona native, she moved to Nashville, Tennessee, four years ago and enjoys exploring Music City at Christmas and all year long. Visit her at LizJohnsonBooks.com or Facebook.com/LizJohnsonBooks.

ANN MATEER ("A Bloom in Winter") has a passion for history and historical fiction, but also has a secret place in her heart devoted to contemporary storytelling. Anne has authored four historical novels and has been a Carol Award finalist and a three-time Genesis Contest finalist. Anne and her husband live in Texas and are the proud parents of three young adults.

JENNESS WALKER ("The Twelve Days of Kindness") lives in south Florida with her Web site designer husband, handsome toddler, and hungry hound. She loves to read, write, decorate, and explore small-town America...and she promises that she never ever sneaked a peek at her Christmas gifts. Check out her Web site at jennesswalker.com.

A NOTE FROM THE EDITORS

We hope you enjoy *A Cup of Christmas Cheer*, created by the Books and Inspirational Media Division of Guideposts, a non-profit organization that touches millions of lives every day through products and services that inspire, encourage, help you grow in your faith, and celebrate God's love in every aspect of your daily life.

Thank you for making a difference with your purchase of this book, which helps fund our many outreach programs to military personnel, prisons, hospitals, nursing homes, and educational institutions. To learn more, visit GuidepostsFoundation.org.

We also maintain many useful and uplifting online resources. Visit Guideposts.org to read true stories of hope and inspiration, access OurPrayer network, sign up for free newsletters, download free e-books, join our Facebook community, and follow our stimulating blogs.

To learn about other Guideposts publications, including the best-selling devotional *Daily Guideposts*, go to ShopGuideposts.org, call (800) 932-2145, or write to Guideposts, PO Box 5815, Harlan, Iowa 51593.